MOPSTERS
BY
Fran Tabor

The Mopsters

F. E. Tabor and Fran Tabor

Published by F. E. Tabor, 2022.

Edited by
Monica Daniels and Christian Von Delius
Cover by
Christian Von Delius

Copyright © 2019 by Frances Elaine Tabor

All rights reserved for any and all mediums. Written permission is required to reproduce, scan or distribute in any printed or electronic form, any part of this book.

F. E. Tabor can be reached at franelainetabor@gmail.com

This book is entirely a work of fiction. Any resemblance to persons living or dead is purely an accident, although well-loved family members and treasured friends inspired many of the names.

This is a work of fiction. Similarities to real people, places, or events are entirely coincidental.

THE MOPSTERS

First edition. July 18, 2022.

Copyright © 2022 F. E. Tabor and Fran Tabor.

ISBN: 979-8201050191

Written by F. E. Tabor and Fran Tabor.

Also by F. E. Tabor

The Mopsters
Eagle Rock

Watch for more at https://www.amazon.com/author/fran-tabor.

Also by Fran Tabor

The Mopsters
To Own Two Suns

Watch for more at https://www.amazon.com/author/fran-tabor.

This book is dedicated to my mother, who taught us the joy of living family love.

Thank you, Mom.

and

To all the many hardworking cleaning women it has been my joy to meet.

This book is dedicated to my mother,
who taught us the joy of living family love.
Thank you, Mom.
and
To all the many hardworking cleaning women it has been my joy to meet.

Table of Contents

Episode 1: Spider Eggs & Zombies!
Episode 2: Mr. Vincent/Cousin Vinny
Episode 3: Lions and Tigers and Tears, Oh My!
Episode 4: Garbage Thieves & Bees—-Ouch!
Episode 5: The Dragon Wakes
Episode 6: Men, Women and Dragons Who Roar
Episode 7: Gimmicks!
Episode 8: Sisters forever, or not
Episode 9: Secrets to Share
Episode 10: Secrets Shared
Episode 11: High Fashion
Episode 12: True Trash
Episode 13: High Class Restaurant Trash?
Episode 14: Up a Tree
Episode 15: Vinny
Episode 16: Mops, Brooms and Bullets!
Episode 17: Kathy's Tale
Episode 18: New Beginnings

Episode 1: Spider Eggs & Zombies!

Elaine complained, "We are late!"

Kaye snapped back, "We wouldn't be late if you drove like a normal person."

Kaye saw her nephew on the school lawn, waiting for them. He wasn't alone. Kaye groaned, "Not again."

Elaine' son, Ahlwynn, stood in front of his teacher, Ms. Charley; both of them statue-stiff.

Elaine's abdominal muscles tightened. "Now what?"

She turned into the school's designated pick-up zone.

As she drove closer, Elaine could tell Ms. Charley grasped her son's shoulder vulture-grip tight. *Most vultures show more compassion than that woman does my son.*

She saw the sheath of papers Ms. Charley held in her other hand.

Elaine parked Rusty-Trusty, her once bright red Subaru wagon, now sun bleached rusty-orange. Elaine had hand painted the front doors white with black letters:

The Mopsters!
The Mopping Sisters!

She took a deep breath; glanced at Kaye. Her sister nodded back. Elaine got out. She walked over to the silent pair.

Forcing friendliness into her voice, Elaine said, "Good afternoon, Ms. Charley."

Ms. Charley said, "This time, you must comply, no more second chances. Your son will go on medication. In all my years teaching, I have never had a child who needed it more."

Elaine asked, "What happened?"

F. E. TABOR AND FRAN TABOR

Ms. Charley said, "He changed the rules at recess, made everyone totally unmanageable—-"

Kaye joined them. "Changed the rules? How?"

Ms. Charley, though shorter than Kaye, managed to look down on her. "Hello, 'Kaye with an E.' I dare say you are a large part of Ahlwynn's problems."

Ms. Charley turned from Kaye, resumed talking to Elaine as though Kaye had not joined them. "We had proper games of catch. I was called to the office. I returned to boys chasing girls, throwing balls, yelling 'Spider Eggs!' and 'I'm an alien!' Some girls writhed on the ground, screaming about spiders in their gut. Others ran pell-mell, screaming even louder."

She glared at Elaine. "What kind of movies do you let him watch?"

Without waiting for an answer, Ms. Charley went on with the next infraction. "I sent him to the principal's office. When Ahlwynn returned, we were about to take a math test. Look!"

Ms. Charley shoved the offending paper into Elaine's face, forcing Elaine to lean back.

Ms. Charlie distracted, Ahlwynn escaped to his Mom's side.

Elaine took the page, held it at arms length, trying to figure out what was on it. Kaye leaned over, stared at the symbol filled page.

Confusing squiggles covered the paper. It took a moment to realize it was a page full of two and three digit addition problems.

Doodles, incorporating all the numbers into the pictures, covered the paper. At first glance it looked like alien ants at a picnic. Wherever there were two zeros together, they were obviously well-endowed lady alien ants.

Kaye sniggered.

Elaine, forcing herself to keep a straight face, said, "Looks like all his answers are right."

Ms. Charley screeched, "You see nothing wrong?"

THE MOPSTERS

Elaine replied, "I haven't checked all the answers, but knowing Ahlwynn I bet none are wrong."

Ahlwynn spoke up. "I did it before hand-in time."

Elaine smiled down at him. "Wow! All the right answers and time for art, too."

Ms. Charley managed to look even more pinch-faced. "If that is your response, I'm not going to waste my time showing you the rest."

She waved the whole wad of papers in Elaine's face. "Just know, any child so out of control he plays leap frog with the desks will not be allowed in my class room. If he can't do what he is told, the way he is told, he is not welcome. I am standing my ground. You get your son proper medical help, and maybe, just maybe, I will let him back in."

Elaine protested, "You don't have the authority to kick him out!"

Ms. Charley said, "Administration agrees with me." She pulled out the bottom paper from the stack, waved it as though it were a battle flag. "This is your formal notification." She handed the official form to Elaine.

Before Elaine had a chance to read it, Ms. Charley thrust the whole bundle into Elaine's hands.

Ms. Charley, holding her head so high her chin practically pointed to the sky, snorted as she turned away and marched back to the school.

Elaine shouted, "He wasn't staying here anyway. Ahlwynn's going to a private school."

Ahlwynn looked up at his mom, eyes wide.

Kaye caught his attention, shook her head no.

Ahlwynn's head drooped.

The three boarded Rusty-Trusty.

Driving home, Elaine and Kaye kept up a running conversation about schools that couldn't recognize genius, didn't appreciate creativity and were not worthy of the children ruined by them.

Ahlwynn stared out the car window, saying nothing, face impassive.

Elaine, glancing at his reflection in the rear view mirror, wondered, *Can a school that destroys my son's spirit, be good for him?*

When the threesome reached home, Elaine tossed the stack of papers onto the couch, the only uncluttered surface in the cramped combination kitchen-dining-living room.

As the two sisters heated up yesterday's leftovers, Ahlwynn sat silent at the table, staring at the ominous stack. *What makes me so bad my teacher never wants to see me again?*

Dinner was put before him; he mechanically picked up his fork.

Elaine noticed Ahlwynn's continuing silence.

ELAINE SHOVED HER SCRAPED-clean plate away from her. "Casserole is always better the next day."

Kaye said, "It sure is. Ahlwynn must agree. That's the most I've seen him eat at one sitting in a long time."

Ahlwynn looked with surprise at his own empty plate. He didn't remember eating. He only remembered staring at the papers; the stack of papers his teacher claimed proved he was unfit to socialize with normal kids.

Elaine smiled. "Ahlwynn, honey, it's so nice out, why don't you go work on your treehouse. Auntie and I will do dishes tonight."

Ahlwynn said, "So you and Auntie can talk about what to do with me?"

Elaine's smile faded. She nodded yes.

"I'm not a little kid anymore. I want to stay."

The two sisters looked at each other.

Elaine said, "OK."

Kaye cleared the table, but left the dirty dishes stacked in the sink.

Ahlwynn gathered up the thick sheath of papers and brought them to the table. *How can something so light feel so heavy?*

They each read every page the teacher sent home with them.

THE MOPSTERS

Ahlwynn said, "It says I can stay until the end of the week as long as we are doing 'due diligence'. What does due diligence mean?"

Elaine answered, "It means that if I make the doctor appointment to get you on 'calming drugs' you have a grace period, you can still attend school as long as no further incidences take place."

Kaye said, "At least it gives us some time until we can come up with a solution."

Ahlwynn looked up at his mom. "Are you going to take me to a doctor?"

Elaine looked serious, put her hand on his forehead. "No temperature."

She felt his arms and legs, "No broken bones."

Ahlwynn giggled.

She looked Ahlwynn in the eye. "I think you are perfect just the way you are. Give me one good reason to take you to the doctor."

Ahlwynn thought *Mom doesn't want some doctor to change me. I don't like being called a freak. But will I be forced to go back?* He said, "Mom, I know private schools cost lots of money and last night I heard you and Auntie talk about late mortgage payments. If I don't go back to school, can I just hang with Cousin Vinny like I did last summer?"

Elaine's eyes widened. "No."

Kaye grinned. "Good idea."

Elaine glared at her sister. "Have you forgotten why I took Vincent off babysitting duty?"

Kaye said, "Vinny promised no more craps lessons or sharing the joys of loaded dice, and there's nothing wrong with playing pool."

Elaine said, "Vincent will never grow up. He's in his thirties and still acts like he did when we were in high school."

Kaye said, "Vinny was fun then, is fun now, and my favorite cousin. You know we can trust him."

Elaine said, "He's our only cousin. Yes, I know we can trust him. Vincent won't let Ahlwynn jump off any bridge he hasn't personally jumped off first."

Kaye said, "You can lie to the school, and hope a miracle happens between now and Friday, or you can stick to your guns, tell them you are not doing any 'due diligence,' and we get Cousin Vinny to watch Ahlwynn during the day since he works nights."

Ahlwynn looked up at his mom. "You say it's bad to lie."

Kaye said, "That's right!" She looked at Elaine. "Sis, you told that *woman*," stressing woman in a way that showed Kaye totally doubted Ms. Charley's claim to any humanity, "Ahlwynn will be attending a private school. You don't get any more private than a personal private tutor."

Elaine threw up her hands. "OK, today is your last day at that zombie-factory school."

Ahlwynn jumped up, started to lurch across the floor, arms out in front of him, "Maybe I want to be a zombie. Brains! Brains!"

Ahlwynn and Kaye laughed.

Elaine did not.

Episode 2: Mr. Vincent/Cousin Vinny

After Ahlwynn went to bed, Elaine called her cousin. "Hello, Vinny? Me, 'Laney."

"Can't talk, at work."

"Vinny, I need you to watch Ahlwynn for a few days."

"What's matter, he sick?"

Elaine paused. "No. He got kicked out of school again, this time permanently."

"Laney, I love the kid and don't mind helpin' a few days, but I ain't no permanent babysitter."

"Vinny, just till I get a few more cleaning jobs. Then I can find a good school for him."

"You still having trouble gettin' jobs that pay?"

Elaine pleaded, "Please."

"I'll be there tomorrow. Maybe a couple more days. Gotta go."

"Vinny, eight-thirty!"

The line went silent.

Elaine turned her phone off. "Hope he heard that."

The next morning Vinny showed up at eight-thirty sharp. At Kaye's relieved look, he said, "What, you doubted me?" He held his hand over his heart. "My feelings are forever hurt."

Kaye said, "Thanks for coming on time. Today's Elaine's turn to drive and she's still dressing."

Vinny said, "Slow as she drives, maybe I should have come yesterday."

Ahlwynn, Vinny and Kaye laughed.

Elaine shouted from her room, "I'm not slow; I'm careful!"

ELAINE SELECTED A PAIR of well-used Levi's from her sparsely filled closet. She averted her eyes from a never-worn pair of 'party Levis' hanging at the far end of the rod. Even in the dark closet, their sequins glittered. *I should have given those things to the Salvation Army years ago; I will never need them. Too bad they're too big for Kaye.* Pulling out her work clothes, Elaine slammed her closet door.

Dressed, she rushed out. "Let's go!"

Ahlwynn looked up from his breakfast cereal. He shouted, "Mom! Your hair!"

Elaine replied, "I'll brush it in the car. We can't be late."

Kaye added, "Simpson's our only paid-up client. Lose her, we lose electricity."

Elaine mouthed to her sister, "*Not in front of the kid.*"

Kaye mouthed back, "*Sorry.*"

Ahlwynn asked, "Problem?"

Elaine mumbled, "She doesn't like my hair either, but it'll be fine. Let's get this show on the road."

Both women hugged Vinny before racing out the door.

Vinny sat down next to Ahlwynn, who just finished his hot cereal. "Did you leave any for your cousin?"

Ahlwynn pointed to the pan on the stove. "Help yourself."

ELAINE CAREFULLY PULLED into the Simpson's driveway. Kaye nervously tapped her fingers on her door handle. "Laney, we are five minutes late. If you hadn't stopped for that long yellow light, forcing us to wait for the next green light, we would have been five minutes early."

THE MOPSTERS

Elaine said, "The important thing is I got us here safely." She jumped out of the car and ran to the back tailgate. "Safety on the road."

Kaye finished their mantra. "Speed on the job."

Elaine grabbed a laundry basket of cleaning supplies from the back of their Subaru while her sister struggled with an armload of brooms, mops and high dusters.

Mrs. Simpson, dressed in sparkling clean gardening clothes, was just exiting her home. "About time! I'm going to help my neighbor with her roses. Start with the kitchen. Be back after lunch. Ta!"

Mrs. Simpson left; the screen door slammed behind her.

Elaine struggled to reopen the door without putting down her overloaded basket. The basket spilled. The door stayed shut. Her hands free, she pushed the stubborn knob and yanked. Propping the door open, she and Kaye picked up the spilled supplies.

Kaye said, "It wouldn't have hurt her to hold the door open."

Elaine said, "She has a lot on her mind. Let's get this over with." They started with their usual check-out walk-through.

Something purple and sticky splattered the kitchen, the hallway, two of children's bedrooms, and even the children's bathroom. The two sisters looked at each other, rolled their eyes, and got to work.

Four baskets of laundry, three grimy picture windows, vacuuming two thousand feet of carpet, and cleaning one massively too full cat box later, the sisters still felt they barely scratched the Simpson-house-grime surface.

MRS. SIMPSON STORMED into the kitchen. "This floor is still filthy! I'm not paying you to sit around!"

Kaye started to say something, but Elaine cut her off before she could finish the first sound. Elaine said, "Good news, we can keep working until five."

Mrs. Simpson snapped, "You're supposed to be finished."

Elaine spoke rapidly. "Mrs. Simpson, as an extra bonus, I can cook one of my famous pot roasts."

Mrs. Simpson looked at both women. "You will not tell anyone you did the cooking."

The sisters nodded.

Mrs. Simpson said, "I presume you saw the roast in the fridge?"

They nodded.

"It better be good." She looked out the window. "My babies just got off the bus. Be finished by the time we get back!" She went running out of the house. "Surprise, darlings! Mommy's got dinner slow cooking! We're going shopping!"

Mrs. Simpson and her two preteen daughters took off in their Escalade.

Elaine and Kaye seasoned the pot roast, cleaned and peeled vegetables and arranged all in Simpson's state-of-the-art slow cooker.

They then finished the playroom, tackled the movie room and gave the living room its finishing touches.

Mrs. Simpson and her daughters returned. "Doesn't Mummy's roast smell good?" Her daughters agreed it did. Mrs. Simpson hollered, "Done yet?"

Elaine carried her full basket of cleaning supplies into the kitchen. "We just finished."

Mrs. Simpson pulled out a sheath of twenties from her purse. She counted out three. "I do hope you don't need an extra two hours next time." She glared at the bundle of mops, brooms and dusters leaning against the door. "What have I said about leaving your junk there?" She started to pull out one of the twenties.

Kaye snatched all three twenties before Mrs. Simpson could finish the action. "Don't worry; we're taking all our junk." Kaye gathered the offending cleaning tools on her way out the door, which she held open with her body while Elaine struggled through with the awkward

THE MOPSTERS

laundry basket, now filled with dirty rags and almost empty bottles of cleaner.

IN THE PRIVACY OF THEIR car, Kaye protested, "I would have made more money working at McDonald's, and worked less."

Her older sister replied, "But no one else would give you free room and board like I do."

Kaye rubbed her shoulder. "Right now, I'm thinking sleeping under a bridge would be a better alternative than going back to that woman's house."

Elaine said, "Add plumbing, and I'll join you!"

Both women laughed.

Both knew when Mrs. Simpson called, they would come running. She always paid cash.

As they rounded the final corner onto their home street, Kaye said, "We should have added extra hot peppers to that pot roast, lots of them!"

Elaine sighed. "If only we didn't need the money."

Kaye asked, "How do other housekeepers get new clients? Ours either have checks that bounce or are demanding fiends. There has—-"

Elaine screamed!

Brakes and tires squealed!

Kaye hit hard against her seatbelt.

Kaye yelled, "What!" She looked around, trying to spot an emergency.

She saw two men carrying a sheet of corrugated metal down the street. One of the men appeared short...

Kaye said, "That's Vinny and Ahlwynn!"

Elaine pulled over to the curb, and rolled down her window. "Vincent!"

Cousin Vinny, holding one end of the discolored old metal roofing material, smiled at his cousins. "Hi! Isn't this about the most beauteous bit of bounty you have ever seen?"

Ahlwynn, his face smudged with soot, grinned at them. "This is perfect! Vinny is going to help me install it!"

Elaine said, "Vincent, where did it come from?"

Cousin Vinny looked down. "Your accusatory tone hurts me, right here." He thumped his chest with his free hand.

Ahlwynn giggled.

Elaine, firmer, "Vincent!"

Cousin Vinny said, "Don't worry. There was a house fire 'bout six blocks over. They're planning to raze it tomorrow, and haul everything to the dump. I got permission to do a little salvage."

Ahlwynn interrupted, "You should see the good stuff we already got!"

Elaine's eyebrows arched upward; her eyes widened.

Kaye laughed. "I can't wait. Beat you home."

Ahlwynn protested, "No fair, you're driving."

Kaye said, "Correction, your Mom's driving."

Vinny said, "True. Ahlwynn, we just might beat them home."

Elaine said, "I'm not slow, just careful. And Ahlwynn——"

"Yes, Mom?"

"Any salvage, what's the rule?"

Ahlwynn replied in a sing-song voice, "Anything you call garbage, goes." His eyes lit up; his grin widened. "Mom all of this stuff is really cool. Just ask Vinny!"

Vinny shrugged his shoulders. "Meet you at the house."

ELAINE SURVEYED THE 'bounty' scattered around the huge old tree that dominated her backyard. A scorched bathroom sink, pipes,

THE MOPSTERS

used wood and numerous unidentifiable bits. *If this stuff doesn't qualify as garbage I don't know what does. It is all going straight to the dumpster!*

Her cousin and son entered through the side gate, proudly carrying the strip of corrugated roofing. They propped it against the back of the ancient, equally useless single stall garage.

Ahlwynn grinned broadly. "Isn't this about the coolest bunch of stuff ever?"

Looking at her son's beaming face, Elaine's resolve faded. "What are your plans for it?"

Ahlwynn ran over to his tree. "Treehouse addition!"

The ancient tree's first branch, so thick it almost qualified as a second trunk, jutted out only inches above the ground. Other branches fanned out like a staircase. Elaine often wondered if her home's first owner had somehow forced the tree to grow in such an artificial fashion. *Did that time-distant person plan for generations of children to see the tree as a stairway to the sky?*

Bits of plywood, scrap lumber and other items salvaged from the neighborhood adorned every branch she could see. Ahlwynn's endless treehouse creations had started innocently enough. So many years ago, when she was reading A Magic Treehouse to her then-toddler son, he had looked up at her, his eyes big with childhood wonder. In the cute piping voice he had back then, he asked, "Mommy, treehouse for me? Please?"

Naturally she had said the only word she wished say to all the things her sweet boy wanted; the word she almost never had the ability to say. "Yes!"

She, Kaye and Vinny installed one small platform, just a little above the ground. Simple. Safe.

Then Vinny introduced Ahlwynn to hammers, nails, and, she suspected, to saws. In the last six years that innocent, safe platform had taken on a life of its own, until now there was as much treehouse as there was tree.

Ahlwynn's voice penetrated the remembering the tree always provoked within Elaine. "...and the sink will go up there."

Cousin Vinny added, "I figured we would work on it tomorrow. It'll be a regular educational experience."

Elaine sighed. "By Friday, any salvage not used in the treehouse, is tossed." She looked firmly at her cousin and son. "Deal?"

Vinny winked at Ahlwynn. They both said, "Deal."

Vinny said, "Speaking of deals, I presume you will pay for my babysitting services by inviting me to dinner?"

"Of course."

DURING DINNER, THE sisters did an exaggerated impression of Mrs. Simpson.

Laughing even harder than his cousins, Vinny said, "You suppose the old b-"

Elaine glared at him.

Vinny continued as though uninterrupted. "Battle ax thought the wicked stepmother was the real hero in Cinderella?"

Ahlwynn giggled. In a high falsetto he sang, "Elaine-ella, Kaye-ella!"

Kaye said, "The worse part is how sometimes she shorts us. Like she tried to today."

Vinny's eyes widened. "I thought she was your high paying client."

Kaye said, "She's the only one who pays us cash every time. The others give us checks. Sometimes we're warned they won't be good for a while; sometimes, we aren't."

Vinny stopped smiling. "Sounds like you need a higher class of clientele."

Elaine said, "But how are we going to find them?"

Vinny sat silent a moment. "There are people who come to the restaurant; they have money. I'll ask around."

THE MOPSTERS

Kaye said, "Vinny, if you know rich clients who will pay us real money....Vinny you know how hard we work, what good work we do, ask, please!"

Vinny looked over at Elaine. "You want I should do that?"

"Yes."

Vinny stood up. "I would stay, help do dishes, but gotta get to work."

Elaine said, "Thanks for watching Ahlwynn. Same time tomorrow?"

"Sure."

Elaine added, "And don't worry about the dishes. Ahlwynn loves helping. Right?"

Her son rolled his eyes as he cleared the table.

VERY LATE AT NIGHT the sound of a ringing phone woke Elaine from a sound sleep.

She croaked into the receiver, "Hello"

A very awake Vincent replied, "Elaine, you awake?"

"Am now."

"Elaine, got you a job, a specialty cleaning, but it's gotta be done tomorrow. You available?"

"Got Mrs. Jensen tomorrow, but she can be put off a day or two. What kind of job?"

"Couple cats got in a fight, left the place a mess. This guy needs it perfect before relatives get home. Will pay ten Franklins if you can do it before five tomorrow."

Elaine woke up completely. "Ten Franklins? A thousand dollars?"

"You want the job?"

"Yes!"

As Elaine went back to sleep, she wondered what kind of cleaning job would pay a thousand dollars.

Episode 3: Lions and Tigers and Tears, Oh My!

Elaine and Kaye drove up the paved driveway. Elaine said, "This looks more like a movie set than a real house. You sure it's the right address?"

Kaye held up the plain white envelope Vinny had given them earlier. An address and a phone number to call when they finished cleaning were printed on its front. It held a key. "It matches."

They parked near the back door. The ornate red cobblestones on the ground felt strange to Elaine as she walked over them.

Everything about the landscaping looked impeccable. The lawn size and ornate shrubbery made it impossible to see any of the neighbors. The house felt as isolated as if it were in the middle of a primeval forest.

Elaine knocked on the door. No one answered. She tried the key. It worked easily.

They entered into a sun room. The morning light streaming through the window lit up a glass-topped, white, wrought iron table. Not a speck of dust showed anywhere.

They went into the next room, a large kitchen with shiny steel and copper pans hanging around a large butcher block work area.

Silently the two women went through an arched doorway, down a hall. They opened a double door.

Bookcases, floor to ceiling on the far wall.

A carved wooden bench, sideways on the floor.

End tables upended.

Broken glass.

F. E. TABOR AND FRAN TABOR

A picture frame, picture torn, on the floor. Shards of glass.
Blood.
Splattered blood.
Walls. Ceiling. Floor.
The women stepped backwards, closed the door.

Elaine and Kaye stared at each other. Elaine opened the door just enough to peek through with one eye. Her sister bent down, peeked into the room at the same time. Their eyes became huge.

They slammed the double door shut; both leaned against it, breathing heavily.

Kaye, whispered, "A cat fight? What kind of cats? Lions?"

Elaine, her fingers shaking, dialed Vinny. "Vincent! There's blood everywhere!"

"I told ya, a couple cats got into a fight."

"There's too much blood for a couple cats. And cats can't knock over furniture."

"They was fightin' a raccoon. Big raccoon. They lost. The animal control people disposed of the bodies, but they ain't no cleaning ladies."

"You should have warned us!"

Vinny asked, "You thought you'd be paid ten big ones for cleaning up after a tea party?" He paused. "You got permission to toss anything broken. Or too dirty to clean."

Elaine clicked her phone off.

Kaye said, "The yard here is so big it's almost a forest by itself. When I took Ahlwynn to the zoo we saw a raccoon bigger than a bear."

Elaine took a deep breath. "I heard raccoons are vicious."

The two women opened the door a crack, took another peak.

Elaine said, "Let's get our cleaning stuff from the car. We will need everything."

Kaye said, "We'll need a big garbage can. I didn't see even a waste basket."

THE MOPSTERS

They carted all their cleaning supplies into The Blood Room; then searched for a garbage can. They found none outside, had no keys to the garage.

Elaine said, "There has to be one in the kitchen. How can you cook without creating garbage?"

They searched the kitchen again.

Kaye, pointing to a one inch hole in the central butcher block kitchen island, said, "Why do you suppose they poked a hole in the middle of the work area?"

The wood grain went flawlessly across the surface, except for the small hole. Elaine looked closer. "I bet you found the missing garbage can!"

She inserted her thumb and lifted the board, to reveal a sink. "Maybe not."

She looked closer; then lifted a section next to the sink. That section covered a stainless steel funnel-shape opening. "Garbage!"

Elaine opened the cupboard door beneath the opening. A heavy duty fifty-five gallon garbage dumpster! Elaine pulled it out; it was empty and clean. The two women dragged it to The Blood Room.

Kaye asked her sister, "Do you think this is the only room the cats fought in?"

Elaine looked at her, her face paled. "We better check."

Glad to have a reason to again leave The Blood Room, they examined the rest of the house, but could find nothing amiss anywhere.

Elaine said, "That's a relief. I don't know if we can finish even this on time."

They swept up glass shards and tossed broken porcelain into the dumpster. Elaine started to scrub the bloody walls. The water turned a sick orange-red. "I need to dump this already. Will you get the back door for me?"

Kaye said, "Don't take it all the way outside. What if it spills? Use the bathroom across the hall."

The bathroom across the hall was so pristine it felt wrong to even think about using it, but Elaine agreed with her sister. It was the only logical choice.

As Elaine poured the bloody water into the commode, a smell like rancid hamburger rose up from the reddish orange water. The blood-stench filled her nostrils. It stirred something deep within her intestines. Her bucket barely emptied, Elaine retched into the orange-water filled commode.

She flushed away the remains of her breakfast. Watching it swirl away with the blood-water made her retch again.

Hearing the noise, Kaye rushed into the bathroom. "You OK?"

Rinsing vomit out of her mouth, Elaine said, "I will never complain about the Simpson cat box again!" Running more cold water, she held her mouth up to the sink faucet, letting the water cleanse her. "That's better." Elaine took a deep breath. "Back to work."

A few minutes later, Kaye dumped her water bucket. She felt just as nauseous, but managed to keep breakfast inside her.

A massive end table proved sturdy enough to stand on for cleaning the few ceiling spots. Both sisters felt relieved that, except for the few blood splatters, the ceiling was cleaner than any ceiling they had ever cleaned before. Most ceilings, you cleaned nothing, or everything, because of the immense contrast between clean and not clean.

Long past noon, Elaine said, "Our lunches are in the car. You hungry?"

Kaye paled. "Do not mention food. Not until after we're home and I've taken a very long shower."

Elaine felt relieved her sister did not want to eat. "You'd think by now the smell and sight of all this wouldn't bother me, but I swear, every time I flush another bucket of bloody water into the sewer, I want to heave after it!"

Kaye nodded. "Me, too."

THE MOPSTERS

HOURS LATER, ALL SIGNS of the animal fight were either scrubbed away or in the large garbage can, except for an upside down end table with a missing leg. The three-legged table top was too large to fit into the dumpster.

Kaye said, "Why don't we throw that into the back of the wagon, and throw it away at home?"

Elaine's eyes widened. Her skin paled. "No way! I'm not putting anything so blood soaked into Rusty-Trusty."

Kaye said, "Rusty-Trusty was ten years old when you bought her. Who knows what she carried then?"

Elaine said, "No, absolutely not."

Kaye said, "We should probably clean it first, in case Ahlwynn can use it in his treehouse."

Elaine's eyes widened even more. "You can't be serious!"

Kaye shrugged her shoulders. "Why not? It is absolutely gorgeous wood, and we were told to get rid of everything broken. We better put it in first, upside down. We can pile our stuff on top of it."

Elaine protested, "All the blood is on the bottom side! One of the cats must have bled to death in it!"

Ignoring her sister, Kaye propped the table onto its side and dragged it towards the kitchen.

Elaine followed her. "What are you doing?"

Kaye said, "I'm not going to mess around with our little buckets of water to clean this thing. There is a perfectly good oversized sink in the kitchen.

Elaine threw up her hands.

Another hour later they had the upside-down, three-legged end table in their wagon, with all their cleaning equipment and supplies loaded on top of it.

Elaine said, "Ready for a final inspection?"

Kaye said, "Ready."

They went in.

The kitchen looked like it had never been used, unless one looked into the cupboard that held the garbage can. That was empty.

The Blood Room was transformed into a spotless genteel library. It looked as though it had never witnessed anything louder than a kitten's gentle purr—-except for the over-full garbage can.

Elaine smiled. "Perfect. All that's left is taking out the garbage."

Elaine grabbed the dumpster's rim, took a deep breath and, with all her weight, jerked the garbage tub towards the door.

It didn't budge.

Her sister joined her. Together, Kaye pushing, Elaine tugging, they forced the overfull garbage dumpster to scrape an inch closer to the door.

Kaye said, "Oh-oh."

"Oh-oh?"

Kaye, pointing to the floor behind the dumpster, said, "Look."

A half inch wide semicircle of scratched wood bordered the shoved garbage can. The dense, light tan gouge contrasted sharply with the dark, well-polished wood floor.

Elaine sighed, "It's too heavy to drag."

Kaye smiled, "We can empty it." She grabbed a large, bloody cushion from the top of the dumpster.

Elaine paled. "And touch all those things again! Worse, it will take hours to carry all this stuff out by hand and it's almost five."

Kaye said, "We need something else to carry the garbage out, and then we can take the can outside and refill it there. We need a wheel barrow."

Elaine yelled, "Our laundry basket." Kaye looked at her sister blankly.

Elaine explained, "We'll carry the larger items, like that cushion, by hand, but everything else we'll carry out in the basket."

THE MOPSTERS

They rushed out to Rusty-Trusty. They pulled out the old laundry basket, dumped it upside down on the ground and ran with it back into the house.

The sisters piled the first layer of bloody garbage from the can into their basket. They then dashed out to the yard; one carrying the basket; the other, larger items. After multiple trips in and out the house, a mound of bloody trash stood in the driveway.

Within seconds of their deadline, the garbage bin had lost enough weight the two women could safely carry it out of the house.

Kaye asked her sister, "Do we salvage our basket?"

Elaine squinched her nose. "Are you kidding?"

Kaye said, "Good!"

Soon the entire mound of filth was piled back into the dumpster, worn out laundry basket perched on top.

Breathing heavily, Elaine leaned against her station wagon and slid to the ground.

Her sister copied her.

Elaine, panting, said, "Ten minutes late, but we finished." She dialed the number on the envelope. It rang multiple times before going to an automatic 'message box not set up' recording.

Kaye said, "Vinny said the homeowner would come here with our pay. Maybe he will just show up on his own?"

A half hour later, they still sat there, still waiting.

Kaye asked her sister, "Do you think we've been stiffed?"

Elaine stared at the smelly, overfull dumpster.

Kaye said, "If we aren't paid, and paid soon, I swear I will take ever bit of that garbage back into the house and make what those cats did look like nothing."

Elaine said "The client must be coming." She frowned. "Unless Vincent..."

Kaye said, "Unless Vincent what?"

Elaine said, "Maybe Vincent didn't give us the right contact information. We could be sitting here, all night, waiting for someone who will never come, while the client is elsewhere, waiting for us to call."

Kaye said nothing, just stared at the overfull dumpster.

They waited.

And waited.

Kaye stood up. "That does it. The garbage goes back in!" She marched towards the dumpster.

Elaine's phone rang with Vincent's ring tone. Elaine answered, "Hello, Vincent. It's past six. The number you gave us is useless and your client still hasn't shown up to pay us."

"That's why I'm calling. He's coming. Now. You done?"

"We're done."

"Good!" He hung up.

Elaine stood up, brushed her hands off and pushed her hair away from her face.

Ten minutes later a long black limousine drove up the driveway, followed by a nondescript pickup truck.

Elaine expected a chauffeur to get out and open the back door. Instead, the driver got out and headed for her. Something about his dress and demeanor reminded Elaine of her bank loan officer.

Two men got out of the pickup's cab. They followed him.

Elaine thought, *Those two look as though they live under one of those bridges Kaye is always joking about.* As the men got closer, the breeze shifted, blowing towards her. *They smell like it, too.*

The well dressed front man said, "My colleagues will stay outside while I inspect your work. May I have the key?"

Elaine handed him the key and followed him towards the house. As they passed the very full garbage can she said, "I didn't want to leave that garbage in the house; it smells too much. This is the can from the kitchen."

THE MOPSTERS

The man nodded, but said nothing. He went straight to The Room.

He walked around it several times. He studied the wall. He got down on hands and knees to inspect the floor and under the benches.

He glanced down at the scratches left from their attempt to remove the too-full garbage bin. Elaine held her breath.

He walked over to the bookshelf, examined the books.

He stood silently in the center of the room, again stared at the floor, then nodded at the two sisters. "You do good work. My family has a specialized cleaning crew, but you did better. Much better." He reached into his pocket, pulled out an envelope; opened it.

He removed a bundle of crisp, new hundred dollar bills, counted them. "...and ten. I believe that is the agreed amount?"

The sisters, speechless at the money, nodded yes.

"I have another cleaning job that needs to be done tomorrow. No wild animals this time, just some messy tenants. It pays the same. You want?"

The sister again nodded yes.

"Good. Here's the address and key."

He handed them another plain white envelope with an address on it and a key inside. "Be done by six. Call your cousin if you finish early."

He led the way out. The women mutely followed.

Outside, he yelled at the two men. "You, put that dumpster in the truck, and buy a new one just like it. Tonight!"

One of the men picked it up, while the other ran to the truck to drop the tailgate. They easily loaded the over-full dumpster into the high truck bed.

The banker-type man turned to the sisters. "What you waiting for? Leave."

They jumped into their car and left.

After no trace of the house, or its neighborhood, remained in the rear view mirror, both resumed breathing normally.

Kaye said, "Did you see how easily those men lifted that can?"

Elaine nodded yes.

Kaye said, "Human gorillas."

Elaine felt a cold shudder go through her body. "I don't ever want to see them again." Her nose crinkled as she remembered their body odor. "The zoo's gorillas are cleaner."

Kaye said, "I'm sure we're overreacting. They didn't say or do anything threatening."

Elaine said, "Trained guard dogs don't talk. They just roll over, sit, heel, and kill."

Elaine pulled into the back of a grocery store. Flies swarmed around a large metal bin filled with rotted food. An open wire enclosure leaned against the store's wall. Cardboard boxes spilled out of it.

Kaye said, "Why are you stopping here?"

Elaine said, "We have to replace our basket."

Kaye said, "Sis, we have a thousand dollars! Let's go to a hardware store and pick up proper totes, with handles. And lids."

Elaine's mouth opened wide, "That's extravagant!"

Kaye said, "You make it sound like buying a Gucci bag! It's an investment, and one that's way overdue."

Elaine glanced at the collection of cleaning supplies strewn in the back of the wagon. "It would be more convenient..."

Kaye said, "Efficient, more efficient. You are always saying efficiency is like giving yourself a raise."

Elaine declared, "You're right! No more dollar store, side-splitting laundry baskets, no more cardboard boxes, we are getting genuine totes."

Ten minutes later the two sisters were pushing a large cart down a hardware store aisle. Elaine whispered to her sister, "I feel tingly just knowing I have the cash to buy almost anything!"

Kaye giggled. "Me, too."

THE MOPSTERS

They finally found the shelf of totes. Elaine reached for the smallest, cheapest one.

Kaye laughed, "That is almost useless. This is what we need!" She grabbed a large, extra deep, sky blue, heavy-duty-plastic wonder of a tote.

Elaine looked at the price tag. "That's more than a week's worth of groceries!"

Kaye grabbed several more. "Mr. Strange is paying us again tomorrow and we will use these for years."

Elaine tried to take the expensive totes from her sister, but Kaye held them firmly.

Kaye said, "You are treating yourself!" She strode towards the checkout.

A variety of extra heavy duty barn brooms bordered the checkout line.

Kaye said, "Elaine, look at these! Their handles are as big around as four of your dollar-store rejects, and feel how stiff and thick the straw is!"

Elaine pointed to the price tags. "I can buy fifty of my brooms for the price of one of these."

Kaye said, "One Mr. Strange job destroyed all the bristles on your wimp broom. We should have left it in the dumpster with the rest of the trash. Look! Five steel bands hold these bristles in place. I bet this broom will survive dozens of gigs like today's." Ignoring her sister, she pulled the best barn broom from the display rack.

Carrying the heavy duty broom in front of her like a royal scepter, Kaye marched up to the clerk.

Elaine followed, protesting all the way. When they reached the counter Elaine pulled out two of the hundred dollar bills.

The clerk reached for the two bills.

Elaine's grasp tightened.

The clerk looked up at her. "Lady, do you want to pay for everything, or not?"

Elaine released her grip. When the clerk counted back the few cents change, Elaine carefully stuffed the coins into her wallet.

Kaye triumphantly carried the new totes and broom to their wagon.

Elaine complained, "A Gucci bag would have been cheaper."

Kaye said, "You would have had only one Gucci and a comb. We have a whole tote set and a real broom!"

WHEN THE SISTERS ARRIVED home, they discovered Vinny had dinner ready for them; hot dog slices baked in macaroni and cheese.

After dinner, Ahlwynn and Vinny both admired the new totes and helped the women arrange all their cleaning supplies in them.

Kaye said, "We have one more surprise waiting in Rusty-Trusty."

Elaine's eyes widened. "No!"

Her younger sister ignored the 'no'. "Come see what is still in back of the wagon." Vinny and Ahlwynn followed her. Kaye opened up the back and pulled out the inverted three-legged table top. She dramatically flipped its top side so that the setting sun lit up its multi-grained wood surface. The sunset's golden light enhanced its many shades of brown far more than had the mansion's harsh electric lights.

Ahlwynn's and Vinny's eyes widened in admiration. They "Ah'ed" together.

Ahlwynn said, "That's bea-u-ti-ful!" He ran his fingers over its smooth surface. Each variety of inlaid wood felt as different from one another as they looked. *With so much finish on it, all those boards should have felt the same, like our kitchen table.* "What are you going to do with it?"

Kaye said, "I thought you could use it in your treehouse."

THE MOPSTERS

Ahlwynn's eye lit up. He looked at his mom. "Can I? Really?"

Elaine nodded yes.

"Oh, wow! Vinny I know just where I want it! Can we do it now, please?"

Vinny inspected the table top. He ran his fingers over its multi-grained surface. "Ahlwynn, you can use those short legs in your treehouse, but this top is quality wood. I have something better in mind for it."

Ahlwynn's smile faded. "Better?"

Vinny nodded yes. "How would you like your very own desk in your room, one just for the story writing you like to do?"

Ahlwynn's eyes went wide. He asked, "You could use this to make a real desk? In my room?" At Cousin Vinny's answering nod, Ahlwynn asked, "Now?"

Vinny laughed. "Not now. Work. Tomorrow?"

Ahlwynn grinned. "Tomorrow!"

AFTER AHLWYNN WENT to bed, Elaine and Kaye sat at the kitchen table. The envelope with the remaining eight hundred dollar bills sat in the middle of the table.

The two sisters stared at the envelope with the same expression they normally used when trying to determine if a moving spot on the ceiling was a friendly bug crawling, or an evil spider lurking.

Elaine said, "Somehow, the banker-looking dude scared me more than the two gorilla men."

Her younger sister nodded agreement. "I don't like how he never told us his name."

Elaine stared at the envelope, but her mind was on the stack of envelopes on her bedroom dresser, each one containing a paper stamped PAST DUE. She looked at her sister. "Perhaps he just doesn't like socializing with the hired help."

Kaye nodded. "Perhaps that's why his two helpers never said anything."

Elaine started to feel better. "I've heard rich people are weird."

Kaye said, "Eccentric. Poor people are crazy; middle class, weird, but if you're rich, you're eccentric."

Elaine said, "Nothing wrong with working for eccentric people."

Kaye said, "Mrs. Jensen! We promised we'd be there tomorrow! Can we put her off another day?"

Elaine said, "I already called her. She started to whine. I told her we decided to not come back until she could pay us in cash, not another check that takes weeks to cash. She said not to bother and hung up."

Kaye smiled. "Looks like a little money gave you some backbone!"

Elaine said, "Or took away brain cells. We don't know how much more work Mr. Strange will have for us and Jensen's checks were always good, eventually."

Elaine took a deep breath. "What should we do with the eight hundred? There are so many places for it to go."

Kaye grinned. "I know the first thing I want to do with it." She grabbed the envelope, pulled out the remaining eight bills, and tossed them into the air. As they fluttered down, she giggled and threw them up again.

Elaine glared at her giggling sister. "Be serious!"

Kaye laughed. "You were on financial death row. You just got a reprieve! Celebrate!" She gathered up the bills and threw them even higher. The green bills fluttered down.

Elaine frowned at her jubilant sister. "There is barely enough to pay last month's mortgage and get the electric company off my back. It's not like we won the lottery!"

Kaye snapped back, "Tomorrow you get another ten lovely pictures of Benjamin Franklin. You've read how celebrities trash places. Maybe some of them don't want the neighbors to know they've had a fight.

THE MOPSTERS

I bet Mister Money Bags has lots of rich friends who will pay us to anonymously clean up their messes."

Elaine rolled her eyes. "One, even two, high paying jobs doesn't change the world." She gathered up the loose bills. "Tomorrow, we visit the bank and the electric office on the way to the new address."

Kaye looked at her sister. "A few years ago, you would have at least smiled. Have you lost all ability to enjoy good fortune?"

Elaine could feel her eyes start to burn the way they did during her secret crying jags. She patted the refilled envelope. "It takes more than money..." Her words trailed away.

Kaye stopped smiling. "It's late. I bet whatever Mr. Strange has in store for us tomorrow is as much work as today. Night, Sis." She escaped to her room.

Elaine called after her sister's retreating back, "Night."

Alone at the table, Elaine sat staring at the fat envelope. Tears ran down her cheek. Her body shuddered. She wished drinking could make her forget, but knew from experience it only made things worse. She grabbed the full Kleenex box from the counter and dashed for the dark privacy of her room.

Hours later her head felt strangely hollow. A pile of well-used Kleenex filled the wastebasket next to her bed. Elaine turned her pillow over, rested her head on its dry side. She fell asleep tightly clutching her pillow.

Episode 4: Garbage Thieves & Bees—-Ouch!

The next morning Elaine sang as she poured pancake batter onto the grill.

Ahlwynn smiled up at her. "The syrup water is bubbling like crazy."

Elaine glanced at the pan of boiling sugar water. "You want to add the flavoring?"

Ahlwynn's smiled broadened. "Yes!" He grabbed the small bottle of maple flavoring and poured a capful of the dark brown liquid into the bubbling sugar water. He watched as the dark brown flavoring swirled into the turbulent water.

Kaye came out of her room. "I smell maple! Must be pancakes!"

Vinny, wearing a vest, came in without knocking. "Homemade hotcakes!" He looked at the table. "Only three places set? What, you going to hurt my feelings again?"

Elaine laughed at him. "Vinny, I didn't expect you early two days in a row. Grab a plate."

Ahlwynn poured the hot syrup into a small ceramic pitcher. "I made the syrup!" He put the container onto the table.

Vinny grabbed a plate and silverware. He helped himself to a cup of coffee before sitting down. "I needed to come early to let you know a few things about your next job."

Elaine paled.

Kaye, taking a sip of coffee, asked, "Such as?"

Elaine flipped pancakes onto each of their plates. She poured more batter before sitting down.

Vinny took his first bite before answering. "Mmmm, even better than House of 'Cakes!" He smiled at Elaine. "If you weren't my cousin, your cooking alone would make me want to marry you."

Kaye laughed. "You like any cooking that's free."

Vincent took a double bite. "Guilty as charged."

Elaine, not smiling, said, "You said there were a few things we needed to know."

Vincent said, "Don't get so worried. Nothing serious. It's just that some kids got a little rowdy. You know, Mom's out of town; Dad's working late. Seems they got to playing darts in the living room, only there ain't no dartboard in the living room, and they were lawn darts. The boss wants ya to find all the holes and patch them."

Elaine said, "I don't know anything about patching holes."

Vincent said, "Don't worry. The room's going to be professionally painted next week. He just needs it to look good this evening. You can plug the holes with toothpaste." He reached into his vest pocket and pulled out several tubes of toothpaste. "Any left over, you keep."

Elaine said, "Why doesn't he just have the painters take care of it today?"

Vincent said, "Duh, didn't I just tell you he needs it to look good tonight? Ya don't want to entertain guests in a room smellin' like paint! 'Sides, even if he could have it painted today, professional painters ain't gonna clean and dust. He wants every piece of furniture cleaned, then polished. Everything. All the books, the knick-knacks, pictures on the wall, everything. And be done by six."

Elaine asked, "Toss out anything broken, like yesterday?"

Vincent, too busy chewing to talk, nodded yes. He swallowed. "How hard could it be?"

Elaine and Kaye looked at each other. Both raised their eyebrows.

Kaye stopped smiling. "Very hard."

Vinny laughed at them.

Ahlwynn said, "Vinny, you said you'd make me a desk today."

THE MOPSTERS

Elaine said, "Ahlwynn, I know Vinny promised he could use that table top to make you a desk, but I checked. Your room's not large enough."

Vinny, wiggling his eyebrows up and down, said in his best Dracula voice, "Don't worry, I have my ways."

Ahlwynn giggled. His mother did not.

KAYE DRIVING, THE SISTERS left.

Elaine stayed silent until they neared the bank. "I don't think it's a good idea."

Kaye asked, "Making a mortgage payment with our loot?" She grinned. "Me neither. We deserve a night on the town. You haven't treated yourself to a good time since forever!"

Elaine, oblivious to Kaye's humor attempt, said, "Mortgage first! Then bills, then, someday, an emergency fund. No partying. I was thinking about Ahlwynn hanging with Cousin Vinny. Vinny's language isn't the best, and the people Vinny hangs out with..." She shook her head. "Maybe I should crawl back to the school, beg forgiveness—"

Kaye yelled, "And let those pinheads turn my nephew into a drugged zombie? No way!" The Subaru's tires squealed as she spun into the bank's parking lot. Kaye slammed the Subaru into the concrete curb stop. "Ahlwynn's not going back!"

Elaine bounced hard against her seatbelt; she screamed, "Watch it!" She took a deep breath. "Sister, that is not safe driving."

Kaye said, "My driving is safer than risking turning Ahlwynn into a zombie!"

Elaine pleaded, "But what choice do I have?"

Kaye said, "Didn't Mom tell us there are always choices, you just have to be open to seeing them?"

Elaine said, "There are no choices when life smashes you like a flyswatter." She stared at the cold, brick monolithic bank in front of them. "Let's go in."

Kaye said, "What happened to my Dragon Lady Sister?"

Elaine asked, "Dragon Lady?"

Kaye said, "When we were little, I thought you were so big, so ferocious, I nicknamed you Dragon Lady."

Elaine said, "You never told me that."

Kaye shrugged, "You don't tell the Dragon Lady you nicknamed her. 'Laney, when we were little you were the bravest kid in the neighborhood. What happened?"

Elaine, still staring at the bank's formidable brick wall, said, "Dragon Ladies are for fairy tales. If life were a fairy tale, then I am Cinderella with a dead prince and a deader fairy godmother." She got out of the car, slamming the door behind her. "Let's get this over with."

Inside they tried to head straight for the teller windows, but the loan officer intercepted them. "Morning, Elaine. Hi, Kaye."

Both ladies mumbled their hellos, and tried to keep going. He stepped in front of them. "Elaine, next week your home will be so far behind, we will have to start—-"

Kaye interrupted him, "My sister's house is worth a lot more than what she owes on it. You take it from her; it's as good as stealing!"

The officer kept talking in soft tones. "That's what I'm trying to prevent. Elaine, list the house, sell it, pocket the money and move somewhere you can afford."

Elaine said, "If the house is worth so much, why can't I just refinance it, get some cash and a lower payment?"

The loan officer sighed. "Be reasonable. There is no way you could ever keep your loan current. You have late fees and penalties. Your debt just keeps growing." He looked forlorn. His voice went to a lower pitch. "Get out before it totally ruins what little credit you have left."

THE MOPSTERS

Elaine held her head higher and turned away from him. "I'm here to make a payment." She saw the smirk on the loan officer's face. *I hope I have enough to get me only two month's behind.* She marched up to the nearest teller's window and handed the young man her payment number. "How much to pay me up to the first of last month?"

"Hmm, with current interest, late fees, penalties, that would be eight hundred, thirty-three dollars and ninety seven cents."

Elaine felt her stomach tighten. *Why did I ask that? Putting only four hundred down will be twice as humiliating!*

Kaye walked up to the window. She spoke loudly, "Here's thirty-four dollars. My sister, of course, has the rest."

Elaine, eyes wide, stared at her sister. She mouthed a silent, "*No!*"

Kaye said loudly, "We don't have all day. Give the man the eight hundred so we can get going."

Elaine handed the teller the envelope. He counted out the money.

Elaine asked, "Our receipt? And could you please tell me how much it will take to be fully caught up."

"Five hundred ninety-five and fifty-seven cents. That's today. Next week, your regular payment will be due."

ONCE IN THE PRIVACY of their car, Elaine shouted at her sister, "You knew I was only going to pay down four hundred! What about the electric bill!"

As Kaye pulled into traffic, she shouted back, "I don't like the way that bank dude's been trying to force you to sell your house." Her voice went sing-song, "There's no way you can ever get current." She tossed her head. "Bank tellers ain't fortune tellers."

Elaine said, "You don't need a crystal ball to see that I've been behind more often than current these past nine years."

Kaye laughed at her, "I don't need a crystal ball to know that tomorrow you will have another ten lovely pictures of Benjamin

Franklin. I can't wait to see the look on that banker's face when you walk in with the money."

Elaine said, "Assuming we get paid in full again, assuming the electric company will wait longer. And assuming taking time out for these jobs doesn't make us loose our regular clients."

Kaye said, "I've got a good feeling about Mr. Strange. I wonder what his real name is."

Elaine said, "You had a 'good feeling' about your last boyfriend."

Kaye said, "At least I had a 'last boyfriend'. It's past time for you to jump back into life."

Elaine shrugged her shoulders. "What do you think we will find at today's house?"

Kaye said, "Hopefully they didn't hit anyone with those darts. I couldn't take more blood."

About a half hour later they pulled up into the driveway. Kaye said, "This neighborhood is positively crowded compared to yesterday's. I can see at least two neighboring houses and I think...yes, there's the roof top of a third neighbor!"

As she got out of her car, Elaine said, "That looks like a brand new garbage can. Any bets it's for us?"

A note on the lid read, *For the Cleaning Crew.*

Kaye frowned. "Does that mean there is an even bigger mess this time?" She paled. "With more blood?"

Elaine said, "Let's check the place out before hauling our stuff in."

This time the back door opened directly into a spacious country style kitchen. Unlike the previous house, a real family obviously lived in this one. Mail sat on the counter, rinsed dishes sat in the sink, a waste basket held recent garbage, with what appeared to be junk mail on top.

Two doors exited the kitchen into the rest of the house.

The closer door opened into a long hallway with five bedrooms. Two of the bedrooms had unmade beds. The other three had such perfectly made beds and nearly empty closets the sisters assumed they

THE MOPSTERS

were guest rooms. At the end of the hallway was a stairway. They walked up.

The upstairs was one large room.

Kaye said, "I thought the rooms downstairs were nice!"

Elaine said, "Wow!"

Kaye said, "Yesterday's house was larger, but this bedroom is nicer than any there."

They tiptoed through the room.

Elaine whispered, "My whole house would fit in here."

Kaye added, "With the yard."

A curved wall partitioned off the master bath area. Both women sighed, "Oh-h-h." The garden tub alone was larger than Elaine's whole bathroom.

Kaye said, "If we finish early, do you think I could sneak in a bubble bath?"

Elaine's mouth dropped open. "You wouldn't!"

Kaye laughed. "I was joking, but...." She wiggled her eyebrows up and down. "Why not?"

Elaine did not return her sister's grin, "Be serious! We are to clean anything that needs it. This area is perfect. Let's go downstairs, make the beds, finish the dishes, and check out the rest."

Kaye, following her sister down the stairs, asked, "How do people make enough money to live like this?"

Elaine said, "I bet they never attended a school like Ahlwynn's."

Kaye corrected her. "Ahlwynn's *old* school."

The second kitchen door led to the public areas of the house. The dining room and family theater rooms were both immaculate. The long, once-ornate living room was not.

Every piece of furniture was upended. Picture frames, glass covers shattered, lay scattered about the floor. Many small dark holes covered the white walls.

Elaine, eyes wide, said, "Is there anything not broken?"

Kaye pointed to the large chandelier dangling in the center of the room. "That's not."

Elaine sighed. "At least there's no blood."

Kaye said, "That we can see. Could be gallons hidden under that mess."

Elaine squinched her nose. "Yuck!" She sniffed. "After yesterday, I will always recognize blood-smell." Elaine sniffed again. "No blood here. Let's grab our totes and bring in the new can they left us."

Kaye said, "I thought you were the smart one. Remember how heavy that dumpster was yesterday? Let's leave the can in the yard and use that waste basket," She pointed to an empty waste can on its side, "To haul out garbage."

Elaine nodded, "Brains run in the family." She looked about the room. "This is a war zone."

The two women quickly cleaned the bedrooms and kitchen.

They re-entered The War Zone. Starting in one corner, they swept up glass shards, gathered broken figurines, and up-righted chairs.

Elaine said, "Sis, I hate to admit it, but your fancy-schmancy broom sweeps so much faster than what we normally use, it might be worth the extra money."

They removed the remaining glass from the picture frames, but left the pictures in them.

Less than half way through Kaye said, "Sis, it's break time. Today I'm hungry."

AS THEY SAT EATING their sack lunches at the kitchen's breakfast bar, Kaye glanced down at the kitchen waste basket. "This looks interesting." She picked up the brochure sitting on top.

Elaine whisper-shouted, "That's private property! Their personal mail!"

THE MOPSTERS

Kaye said, "What's personal about garbage? Besides, look what it says on top, *Please share with your friends.* It's an open-house invitation for the private school their kids go to. Thanks to me, it's being shared."

Elaine protested, "The school did not have garbage-raiding cleaning ladies in mind when they talked about inviting friends to the open house. And how do you know the kids in this house go there?"

Kaye shrugged her shoulders. "It's obvious. Didn't you see the open tuition bill on the counter?" She folded the brochure and stuck it in her pocket.

Elaine, eyes wide, "You can't take that!"

Her little sister blinked her eyes to feign innocence. "Why? It's no different than taking the broken table yesterday."

Elaine protested, "But I planned to toss the table."

Kaye said, "I promise, this paper," She patted her pocket. "Will end up in the garbage. Eventually."

Elaine said, "Perhaps we should dump out this wastebasket and wipe it down, just to be thorough."

Kaye laughed at her older sister. "Sounds like you are trying to hide the evidence I stole some trash."

―――※―――

THEY SPENT THE NEXT five hours cleaning The War Room. By the time they were done, the outside garbage can had debris piled high above its rim; three over-filled waste baskets stood next to it, and a badly broken chair lay next to them.

Finally, they could start filling in all the small round holes with toothpaste as per their instructions.

Elaine's cell phone rang.

"Hello"

"'Laney, you done yet?'

"No Vince. We have at least an hour's worth of hole filling to do."

"An hour! Boss man's heading their now!"

Elaine said, "Call and tell him to wait a little; we can't work any faster."

Vincent said, "He's not the type to take calls. Hurry!" He hung up.

Elaine turned to Kaye. "Hear that?"

Kaye nodded yes as she grabbed another tube of toothpaste. "You finish up here; I'll work on the next wall. Let's concentrate on everything eye level and then go back if we have time."

Each sister soon found her own rhythm. Find a hole; plug it up, blend it in. Find the next hole; fill it up, blend it in...

Neither noticed a car driving up to the house.

Neither heard the kitchen door open, footsteps coming down the hall or the door to The War Room open.

A deep voice boomed, "You were told, 'be done by six.' It is six-thirty."

Elaine dropped her tube of toothpaste; turned to the intruder. It was Mr. Strange.

Relieved, Elaine said, "Oh, you!" She picked up the tube and filled another hole. "We need more time. At least an hour."

Mr. Strange said, "You got fifteen minutes. Being late, you forfeit a hundred."

Kaye demanded, "You promised a thousand! You better pay the full amount, or—"

Mr. Strange turned towards Kaye. His gaze drifted from her head to her feet, then slowly back to her head. His words as slow as they were precise, "You threatening me?"

The girls looked at each other, eyes wide. Both, talking over each other with nervous speed, "No, not at all." "You were so late yesterday..."

Mr. Strange stood silent until their protest petered into silence. His voice even lower pitched, his words deliberate, "My time is my concern. Your concern is working when you say you will work, and finishing when I say. If you had not stopped at the bank first, you would have been done now."

THE MOPSTERS

Elaine felt a shiver run down her back. *How did he know?* She said, "I had to stop."

Mr. Strange looked at his watch. "Fourteen minutes."

Both women plugged holes.

Mr. Strange walked around the room. He scrutinized the floor, the furniture, the few shelves. He noted the high holes not yet filled; the few near the floor. "You got a ladder?"

Elaine said, "No."

He spoke into his cell phone.

In less than a minute the same two henchmen who came with him the day before entered carrying a ladder. Judging from their aroma, they still hadn't bathed.

They gave the ladder to Elaine.

Mr. Strange said, "Now you have a ladder."

Elaine set the ladder up beneath the high holes. She started to climb.

The ladder wobbled. She clutched the sides so tightly her fingers turned white.

"I can't go any higher."

Mr. Strange questioned, "Can't?"

"The ladder's not stable."

Mr. Strange snapped his fingers. The two henchmen rushed to the ladder and held it tight. "Now it's stable. Finish."

Elaine looked at the faces of the men holding the ladder. Not friendly. Their body odor wafted upward. Her stomach, already queasy at the thought of going higher, became queasier.

Elaine made eye contact with one of the men. *I've heard of men who could undress you with their eyes. His eyes suggest skinning.* Fear overrode queasy. She rushed to the top of the ladder.

At the sound Kaye glanced over. *Elaine, on a ladder? On its TOP step!* Kaye's eyes went round; her mouth dropped open.

Mr. Strange shouted, "You, Little Sister, keep working! Faster!"

Little sister Kaye worked faster.

Twenty minutes later the two sisters stood in the middle of the room while Mr. Strange walked slowly around the room, giving the walls a final inspection.

He returned to the two women and pulled a white envelope from his inside suit pocket. He deliberately pulled a single hundred dollar bill from it, shoved the bill back into his suit pocket, and then counted out the remaining nine bills. He replaced the nine into the envelope and started to hand the cash to Elaine.

Kaye stepped forward, her arm blocking Elaine. "No you don't!"

Elaine paled.

Mr. Strange glared. "You finished late."

Kaye stared into his eyes. "You said to clean and straighten out everything that needed cleaning. We didn't do just this room. We made beds, cleaned bathrooms, did dishes. We even took out the stinking kitchen garbage!"

Mr. Strange blinked. He turned to one of the henchmen. "You, check."

The man left. A few minutes later he returned and nodded to his boss.

Mr. Strange reached into his pocket and pulled out the tenth hundred. "This time, doing a deluxe job makes up for being slow. But don't think I will be so generous again."

He replaced the tenth bill into the envelope. He handed the full thousand dollars to Elaine.

Elaine said, "Thank—-"

Mr. Strange cut her off. "Leave. Now."

They left. Fast.

Only after they finally merged into the interstate did the two women relax.

Elaine asked, "Do you still have a 'good feeling' about Mr. Strange?"

THE MOPSTERS

Kaye said, "About him...undecided. But about *this*," She tapped the brochure she was reading. "You bet!"

Elaine said, "That is a stolen—-"

Kaye said, "Puh—leaze! It is salvaged, not stolen! Listen to this. 'Kathy's School is looking for families who want to both maximize their child's learning potential and their creativity!' It talks about how they teach learning by doing. Elaine, it sounds exactly like the kind of school Ahlwynn should attend!"

Elaine said, "The tuition *is* exactly what Ahlwynn's mother should be able to pay, but can't."

Kaye said, "You don't mind window shopping for shoes you can't afford."

Elaine said, "Walking away from lovely but overpriced footwear doesn't hurt. Walking away from a school Ahlwynn might love, that would hurt." She heard Kaye's cell phone beep-beep-beeping. "What are you doing?"

Kaye waved her sister off. "Hush, I'm on the phone!" Her tone changed to sugary sweet. "Hi, I just learned about tonight's open house. Is it too late to RSVP?"

Pause. "Yes."

Pause, "Upper Elementary."

Pause. "Perfect. My sister's Elaine and I'm Kaye; that's Kaye with an E."

Pause. "Ahlwynn, and no food allergies."

Pause. "Thank you. We'll be there."

Elaine glared at her sister. "How dare you promise I will go somewhere without asking me first! Worse, why expose Ahlwynn to something he can't have?"

Kaye shouted back, "You have been walking away from things and people for ten years. It is time you rejoined the land of the living, even if it means getting hurt."

Elaine said, "I keep only who and what's important. You, Cousin Vincent, Ahlwynn. The house."

Kaye said, "Since Ahlwynn's birth you haven't taken up one new hobby, made one new friend or even had a new haircut! Years ago you used having an infant son as an excuse. Now your excuse is being broke. The reality? My big, brave older sister is a coward. I want Dragon Lady back."

"I'm prudent, not cowardly."

"Coward!"

"Am not!"

"Prove it! Go to the Kathy's School open house! Talk to at least one other person there. Not just any person, a man without a ring!"

Elaine's face paled.

WHEN THEY ENTERED THEIR driveway, Ahlwynn ran out of the house. "Mom, Auntie, come see what Vinny made!"

As Elaine got out of the car, Ahlwynn grabbed her hand and practically dragged her into the house and to his room. Kaye followed.

Ahlwynn flung the door open, "Ta-da!"

The fancy table top hung on the wall, its bottom side facing outward. Ahlwynn ran into the room. He released two hooks on either side of the table. The table, hinged to the wall and supported by two chains, lowered to create a flat desk. Ahlwynn jumped onto his bed and slid over. The desk was perfectly aligned to use the bed as a chair. Ahlwynn beamed up at the two women. "Is this cool, or what?"

Elaine and Kaye laughed.

Elaine said, "Very cool."

Vinny came up behind them. "You didn't know your dear old cousin Vinny had such talents, did you?"

Kaye ran her hand over the shiny, multi-shaded inlaid wooden panels. "You are so right. This wood is too beautiful to leave outside."

THE MOPSTERS

Vinny said, "Speaking of beautiful, I just finished baking a culinary masterpiece designed to delight the eye as much as the palette."

Elaine and Kaye looked at each other. In unison they said, "Hot dogs and—-"

Ahlwynn chimed in. "Macaroni!"

AS THEY ATE DINNER, Kaye showed Vinny and Ahlwynn the school brochure. "...the best part is, we get to go to the open house tonight!"

Ahlwynn asked, "Me, too?"

Vinny said, "Of course you too. If you like the joint, we will consider letting them take you on. If you don't like it, no way we gonna let them have you!"

Ahlwynn asked, "Vinny, you coming?"

Vinny started to speak but Elaine cut him off. "Cousin Vinny works tonight."

Ahlwynn asked, "Aren't schools like this expensive?"

Elaine said, "Yes—-"

Kaye interrupted, "But they have scholarships, work-study, and other payment options."

Ahlwynn's eyes grew round. "You mean there might be a way..."

Vinny stood up. "First you find out if you want it. Just because something sounds good," he pointed down at the brochure. "Doesn't mean it's worth a plug nickel." He headed for the door. "Time to work!"

CARS FILLED UP THE school's small parking lot and spilled out into the narrow, tree-lined street.

As they walked to the school Kaye said, "Two blocks! The closest spot is two blocks away! Proof positive this is a great school!"

Elaine said, "Or proof it's so expensive it takes three or four working adults to pay the tuition and everyone brought his own car."

Kaye said, "Maybe it's so good, the parents are showing off the school to everyone they know."

Light poured out of all the windows. Two young students stood by the door, forcing brochures on all who entered.

A boy about Ahlwynn's age came up to them. "Hi, is this your first visit?"

Elaine said, "Yes."

He smiled broadly, "I'm Tim. May I be your guide?"

Elaine questioned, "My guide?"

The boy answered, "If you have never been here before, Kathy's School can be confusing. As your guide, I will show you everything from our preschool classrooms to the science labs."

Elaine said, "Ahlwynn, we should go straight to your grade's classroom."

Tim said, "We don't have grades. We have three year age groupings, but we aren't stuck in just one classroom. Sometimes a kid will work with younger or older kids for special projects. Like right now I'm helping little kids learn to read and I'm helping some older kids build a robot we're going to enter into a state competition." He looked at Ahlwynn. "I bet you would be in my class, the one for ten, eleven and twelve year olds."

Ahlwynn grinned. "Yep! Let's check out the robot!"

Elaine interrupted her son. "Classroom first."

※

THE CLASSROOM WAS NOT like any classroom Elaine had ever seen. A large area rug dominated the room. Smaller braided rugs were

THE MOPSTERS

scattered around. Several children playing with blocks and beads sat on the smaller mats.

A few old fashion student desks were lined up in front of the window. A large, plastic, avocado green bean bag chair, surely the ugliest bean bag she had ever seen, leaned against the wall. Shelves filled with plastic bins, models and books lined every wall, including the two walls that jutted out beneath a corner loft. A wall-mounted ladder led up to the loft. Wooden rods bordered the loft like the bars of a jail cell.

Elaine frowned as she looked at the ladder. *That thing goes up at least six feet! I bet the ceiling up there is only about four feet high. It looks like a big bird cage. Is it a punishment space, for time outs?* She looked away and focused on the children safely sitting on the floor. Elaine asked, "What are they doing?"

Tim said, "Those kids are showing how we learn with hands-on materials."

Elaine thought, *It looks like preschool work. No way will my son go here.*

Ahlwynn pointed to the corner loft. "What's that?"

Tim said, "That's our thinking corner. Come see!"

He ran over to it and scrambled up the ladder. Ahlwynn followed.

Elaine held her breath until her son made it to the top and disappeared into the small loft.

Kaye followed the boys up. "'Laney, you have got to see this!" She slid into the small space.

Elaine gripped the ladder's side bars tightly. Slowly she stepped onto the first rung, then the second. After several steps she was able to look into the loft.

Her sister, son and Tim were sprawled out on a thick white rug. The shelves held a few books, clip boards, stacks of blank paper and jars of pens, colored pencils and crayons. Ahlwynn grinned. "Mom, isn't this the coolest room ever!"

Elaine thought, *Should I force myself to join them or—-*

Before she could finish her thought, a bee buzzed her head. She brushed it away.

The bee stung her.

Elaine screamed. She fell backwards.

Into a man's arms.

She could feel him dip down slightly when he caught her.

He held her secure. Her head leaned against his chest and shoulder. *Man scent, good man scent. Smells... safety.* She tried to tell herself safety did not have a smell, but her body screamed otherwise.

He allowed her body to gracefully land feet first, but kept his strong arms around her torso.

Elaine looked up into a very masculine face, a face filled with concern. A face with dark eyes. Deep, dark eyes. Eyes to get lost in.

Pain filled her.

Elaine heard thump, thump, thump as the three from the loft jumped onto the floor.

The man said something.

Elaine heard warm vibrations, thick with all the overtones only a man's voice could possess. She said, "Huh?"

"ARE YOU ALL RIGHT?" The man glanced at the woman's rapidly swelling arm. "You're not! Tim! Ice bag!"

He lifted her onto the bean bag. The woman collapsed into it. It was easy to tell where the hornet had stung her.

ELAINE FELT STRONG hands examining her. She felt pressure; the stinger popped out.

Her sister's voice. Something about venom. Her son's cry. The world faded.

THE MOPSTERS

ELAINE SAT UP IN THE ugly bean bag chair. *What?*

"Mom, you're alright!"

Kaye said, "You are lucky this school is prepared for just about everything!"

Elaine looked at her puffy arm. "Most bee stings don't affect me." She looked around. A tall, broad shouldered man in an off-white windbreaker, his back to her, stood by the windows. *Is that him? Is he real?*

The man turned around.

It's him!

He spoke, "It wasn't a bee. It was a hornet. Every time you get stung, you risk becoming more sensitive. You better start carrying Benadryl with you."

Elaine nodded.

He continued, "Your sister said she would drive you home."

Elaine shook her head. "I'm OK enough to drive."

Ahlwynn, his eyes red, said, "You really OK, Mom?"

Elaine smiled at her son. "Really-o, truly-o, OK."

Ahlwynn grinned broadly, "Then you've got to see the rest of this school. It is so-o-o cool! Mom, it has got to be the best, funnest school ever!"

Elaine said, "Fun isn't everything."

Kaye said, "Sis, don't jump to conclusions. Edward's been telling me about this place."

Elaine asked, "Edward?"

Kaye, her eyes opening a bit wider, said, "The man who caught you."

Elaine's thoughts hit faster than the bee's stinger had stabbed her. *I've seen that* this-man-is-the-one *look in your eyes before. Don't blame you. He's easily the cutest guy I've seen since...* Elaine blinked hard. *It's been over ten years, more than enough time...* Another hard blink. *Edward... A strong name, as strong as the man who bares it... A man my sister finds attractive.*

Elaine's throat constricted with pain that had nothing to do with the bee sting. *Sis, I love you, but your sexy size eight body makes my jumbo-sized self invisible to men.*

Aloud Elaine said, "Talk? How long was I out?"

Ahlwynn spoke up, "It seemed forever, but the medicine made your swelling go down almost immediately and your breathing went normal in a minute. Auntie Kaye said you stayed asleep so long because you're sleep deprived."

Edward said, "You reacted so fast to the bee sting, I called an ambulance. The paramedics agreed with your sister."

Elaine frowned. "Paramedics? Ambulance? Weren't there sirens?"

Ahlwynn spoke up. "Were there ever!"

Tim, their guide, came over. "This is the most exciting open house we've ever had!"

Elaine looked around. "Where is everyone?"

A strange lady joined them. "Glad you're feeling better. I'm Kathy, Edward's sister, the head teacher for this class and the school's founder. The open house finished about a half hour ago."

Elaine stood up. "I'm so sorry! We'll be going."

Kathy said, "Don't be! If it weren't for the bee sting I wouldn't have had a chance to talk with your son. He's easily one of the most creative children I've met in a long time."

Elaine said, "Perhaps too creative. He—-"

Kaye interrupted her sister. "Edward told me this school has scholarships and work-for-payment plans. He also said this school 'maximizes potential.' That's academic code for helping kids be way smarter than in public school." She smiled at Edward. "He really cares about children."

THE MOPSTERS

Edward smiled back. "My sister has shown me some of the work done by the 'incorrigibles' in her classroom. If I could have attended a school like this, I wouldn't have had so many calls home about my latest shenanigans."

Kathy laughed at him. "Ed, I think even my school would have had trouble with the boy you were!"

Edward reached into his pocket, pulled out a business card. He looked directly at Elaine. "Give me a call if you have any more questions, or if you get worse. I can give you a ride to the hospital a lot cheaper than an ambulance."

Edward started to hand Elaine his card, but Kaye snatched it. "Elaine has trouble keeping track of things." She smiled at Edward and slowly blinked her eyes. "I'll call you tomorrow with a progress report."

Edward said, "Just to be on the safe side, perhaps I should give a card to both of you." He handed a second card to Elaine.

Elaine took the card. "Edward Wachholt. Consultant." She winkled her forehead. "Shouldn't you say what kind of consultant?"

Kathy said, "Eddy is an expert on everything."

Elaine said, "Really?"

Edward's lips turned up slightly. "It's true; some of my clients insist I must be an expert on everything because I 'never fail to give good advice'. The reality?" He shrugged his shoulders. "I'm the kind of consultant who asks questions until you come up with your own answers. The only thing I'm really an expert at is asking questions."

Elaine said, "I've heard that to ask the right question you have to almost know the answer. If true, you are an expert on everything."

Edward laughed, "How about an almost-expert on almost everything?"

Kaye said, "Edward, I bet you are like a lot of bachelors and seldom get home cooked meals. How about coming to our place tomorrow for dinner? You can get a home cooked meal and check on my sis to make sure she hasn't had a relapse."

F. E. TABOR AND FRAN TABOR

Kathy started to say something, but Edward cut her off. "Great idea. What time and where is dinner?"

Episode 5: The Dragon Wakes

Driving home, Kaye blathered so excitedly about Edward that she didn't noticed both her young nephew and older sister did little more than "uh-uh" their responses.

Elaine, a thick pile of papers in her lap, sat silent. *Kaye's last boyfriend was only a month ago. I haven't met anyone I find even remotely attractive until tonight. Why do all men want cute and tiny? And these registration papers! Kaye's getting my son's hopes up just to get them dashed to the ground!*

Aloud, Elaine snapped, "Why did you tell Kathy we will enroll Ahlwynn? Even with half the tuition paid with scholarships and work programs, there is still no way I can afford that school."

Kaye rolled her eyes. "Sis, you have got to learn to have faith! If we get just one cleaning job a week from Mr. Strange, you'll easily afford that school."

Elaine sighed deeply. "Mr. Strange has not promised us more gigs. How often can he need a thousand dollar cleaning? Counting on him is like counting on the lottery. Just plain stupid!"

Ahlwynn interrupted the two sisters. "Mom, what if I help you clean people's homes? Could that help you work faster and get more jobs?"

Elaine said, "You're a kid. You're supposed to be enjoying kid things."

Ahlwynn said, "I really want to go to this school. I'm old enough to help."

Elaine said, "You're not even a teenager!"

F. E. TABOR AND FRAN TABOR

Ahlwynn said, "Benjamin Franklin was working full time at my age!"

The sisters looked at each other. Kaye asked, "Is that true?"

Elaine answered, "I don't know. But that doesn't change a thing."

Ahlwynn said, "Does to! All the great men say the same thing. If you don't want something bad enough to work for it, you don't want it!"

Elaine said, "I don't——"

Ahlwynn added, "If I'm working with you, Cousin Vinny won't have to babysit me!"

Kaye stifled a giggle as her sister said, "OK, we'll give it a try."

Ahlwynn grinned. "I'm going to school! I'm going to school!"

Elaine said, "You've gone to school before."

Ahlwynn said, "That was a Zombie Factory."

Elaine said, "And this one is?"

Ahlwynn grinned, "An awesome learning explosion with robots!"

Kaye smiled back. "A direct quote from tonight's tour."

Elaine frowned. "It takes a two thousand five hundred dollar deposit. As soon as we get that saved up, I will register you."

Ahlwynn said, "With my help, we'll get that money in no time!"

THE NEXT MORNING THE three of them showed up at Mrs. Greene's house. She looked down through her bifocals at Ahlwynn. "What's he doing here?"

Kaye spoke up. "He doesn't have school today, so we thought we'd let him help."

Mrs. Green pursed her lips, frowned and said, "Young man, no roughhousing. You understand? I know how boys can get roughhousing, breaking things, yelling."

Elaine said, "You needn't worry, Mrs. Green. He is here to help me."

THE MOPSTERS

Mrs. Green backed away from the door, allowing the trio to enter her home.

Ahlwynn smiled up at her. "I have things I wouldn't want anyone to break, too. I will treat everything you have like it was my very best model."

Mrs. Green smiled at him.

An hour later, Kaye said to Elaine, "We should have had Ahlwynn help us before."

Elaine nodded. "Listen to that vacuum cleaner hum."

The smooth sound of Mrs. Green's vacuum cleaner could be heard through the wall while they cleaned the master bathroom. When finished, they moved to the next room. The sound of the vacuum naturally faded.

About an hour later Kaye said, "Shouldn't Ahlwynn be finished vacuuming?"

Elaine answered, "Yes, he should already be asking me what to do next." She frowned. "Mrs. Green has more knick knacks on display than any store in town. You don't suppose..."

"Let's check!"

Leaving their cleaning supplies behind, they searched for Ahlwynn. The carpeted halls, sewing room and living room carpets all looked freshly vacuumed, but they couldn't find Ahlwynn. Elaine said, "What could have happened?"

As they went past the kitchen, Kaye asked, "Is that giggling?"

They looked into the kitchen. No one. They heard Ahlwynn's voice. "That's when I got The Idea—-"

Elaine yelled, "Ahlwynn, where are you?"

"Outside!"

The sisters went out the back door. Ahlwynn sat at the patio table with Mrs. Green. A big plate of cookies and a glass of milk sat in front of him.

Mrs. Green did something neither sister had seen her do before. She smiled a full teeth-showing smile. "He did such an excellent job of vacuuming; I just knew he needed a break."

Elaine said, "He's not to bother you."

Mrs. Green laughed. "He is no bother. Young Ahlwynn reminds me of my brother! My brother wanted to be a real life Robinson Crusoe, too."

Elaine said, "Then you don't mind him coming with us?"

Mrs. Green sat up straighter. She quit smiling. "But I do mind. I mind a great deal. Anyone as bright as young Ahlwynn deserves to be in school. Elaine, if you do not get him into a school commensurate with his abilities, you are a terrible parent and I will report you!"

Elaine's face reddened. "Y—-"

Kaye interrupted, "Don't worry, Mrs. Green. We finally found an excellent school that will allow my nephew to reach his full potential. We will enroll him Monday."

Ahlwynn's eyes went wide. "Mom said—-"

Kaye interrupted, "She wanted to keep it a surprise."

Ahlwynn jumped up and hugged his mother. "Wow! Thank you!"

Mrs. Green's smile returned. "Wonderful. You two finish cleaning while young Ahlwynn and I converse." Ignoring Elaine and Kaye, she turned back to Ahlwynn. "Tell me more about that school."

Driving home, the sisters sat in up front. Ahlwynn sat in back reading.

Kaye said, "Let's stop at the market to get fresh lettuce for the salad."

Elaine glared at her. "Why, so we can show off for your new boyfriend?" Her voice went into a high-pitched, exaggerated southern accent. "Why Eddy, darling, we're serving a delightful garden fresh salad followed by a gourmet Italian Surprise for your dining pleasure. Would you prefer Rothschild '61 or '72?"

THE MOPSTERS

Kaye shouted at her. "What is wrong with you? You act like a little lettuce is the ultimate show-off!"

Elaine shouted back, "You should never have invited him! We both worked hard all week, it would be nice to kick back and relax. But no, we will barely have time to do a speed-up spruce-up for our own place tonight while dinner simmers, make a proper salad, and you want to take even more time shopping! If that's not enough, I just remembered the bathroom is definitely not company ready!"

Kaye said, "He's not coming to check out our cleaning skills. He's coming to check out your health!"

Elaine snapped, "Call him up and tell him I am healthy enough to clean houses, lots of houses, everybody's house but my own!"

Kaye exclaimed, "You really don't want Eddy to come to dinner!"

Elaine said, "Of course not! The house is a mess. I'm a bigger mess! And it will be embarrassing when…" Elaine suddenly went silent.

Kaye looked blank. "Embarrassing?"

Elaine mouthed, *Quiet!* She pointed to the back seat.

On cue, Ahlwynn lifted his nose out of the book. "What would be embarrassing?"

Elaine said, "Not being able to make a proper first impression."

Kaye said, "You never worry about impressing my boyfriends."

Elaine said, "He's not your boyfriend, he's…" Elaine paused a micro second longer than normal. "The teacher's brother."

Kaye said, "All the more reason to get fresh salad fixings."

Elaine protested, "There's not enough time."

Ahlwynn said, "If Edward's early, I can show him my tree-house until you say it is safe to come in."

Kaye grinned. "Fresh salad."

An hour later they finally pulled up into their own driveway. An unfamiliar white sedan was parked in front of their home; Edward leaned against it, arms folded. The pit of Elaine's stomach tightened.

F. E. TABOR AND FRAN TABOR

He's early! My hair's a mess, my clothes are stained, and my face hasn't seen makeup for years.

When Elaine exited Rusty-Trusty, she could see Edward better. She noticed how tightly the short sleeves of Edward's bright yellow polo shirt clung to his bulging biceps. *I knew he was strong from the way he carried me. I had no idea how well built...He's even better looking tonight...* She felt her thigh muscles tighten.

Kaye jumped out of the car. "Eddy!"

Edward smiled at her. "I started to believe you stood me up." He noticed Ahlwynn carrying a grocery bag. Elaine opened the Subaru's other back door and started to grab a second grocery bag. Edward dashed over to her. "Let me carry that." He took the bag from her. "Are there any more?"

Elaine smiled up at him. "No."

Edward said, "Since you're just getting home with the groceries, does that mean I get to show off my kitchen skills?"

Kaye stepped between them. "No. You get to let us show off our skills!"

Ahlwynn said, "As soon as we unload these sacks in the kitchen, I'm going to keep you busy showing you my treehouse!"

Edward followed everyone into the house, a big smile on his face, but his darting eyes caught every detail.

He could easily tell from the outside the house was small, but the reality of the tiny kitchen area shocked him. He didn't have to ask where to put his grocery bag. The few inches of empty counter space on either side of the double sink could not handle more than a coffee cup. The other wall was all stove and refrigerator. He put the grocery sack in the middle of the rectangular steel table. A steel chair was pushed against each of the three nearest sides of the table; the patterns on their vinyl backs faded into invisibility. A fourth matching chair sat nearby.

The short side of the table was near the sink. The longer side of the table paralleled the white stove and refrigerator. *There is barely enough*

THE MOPSTERS

room for the ladies to walk between the table and the appliances, and definitely not enough for me. No wonder there is no chair on that side.

A small over-stuffed love seat, its back to the kitchen table, separated the equally small living area from the kitchen. A TV sat opposite the little couch. A bookcase crammed full of books, papers and small boxes leaned against one wall. An open door next to the bookcase revealed a white sink, obviously the bathroom. There was no other furniture.

The 'official' front door on the far wall looked as though it were never used. The wall opposite the bathroom held three doors. Judging from their spacing, and what he already knew of the outside of the house, Edward correctly deduced two of the rooms were about the same size and the third room must be much smaller, more closet than room. He would have thought it was a closet, except its open door revealed a narrow, unmade bed.

As he put his bag down Edward said, "I can chop onions with the best of them. Sure you don't want my help?"

In unison, both sisters said, "No!"

Ahlwynn said, "Remember, it's my job to keep you busy while they cook and clean."

As soon as her son had Edward safely away into the backyard, Elaine turned on her sister. "It will take me months to save enough for just the registration. You as good as promised my son he will start going there next week! Ahlwynn's going to be crushed! As if that's not enough, we need to look good if that place will even consider a scholarship. Do you have a clue how flaky we will look when Edward finds out just how broke we are, how we had no business even stepping foot in that school's open house? Flaky people don't get scholarships!"

Kaye laughed at her. "By the time Edward discovers we're broke, he will be so dazzled by your cooking and my..." Kaye rolled her shoulders, flipped her hair and wiggled her hips. "Ooh-la-la! He won't even care!"

She grabbed the vacuum. "I'll clean while you cook, deal?" She started vacuuming. The machine's high-pitched whine filled the room.

Elaine said, "Edward's not the easily blinded type." Her sister never heard her.

───⋅⟡⋅───

EDWARD HAD NEVER SEEN a tree quite like the one that dominated the small back yard. Its first branch was only a few inches above the ground. Other branches radiated out and upwards like a lighthouse staircase. It looked as though a tribe of hoarders lived in the tree.

The bottom two branches supported a wooden platform; more platforms were mounted on upper branches. Edward looked up into the tree so sharply he could feel his neck protest. His eyes tried to make sense of the confusion above. Bits of sheet metal, carved furniture legs, broken shelves, even—-at least twenty feet up—-a sideways mounted sink. All tied, nailed, screwed or wedged between and on branches.

Ahlwynn, grabbing a branch above his head, pulled himself up and disappeared behind some planks. He shouted, "Follow me!"

Sure his tall frame would never be able to execute the contortions necessary to get very high in the tree, Edward followed. He discovered if he followed Ahlwynn's route he had just enough clearance to wedge between the branches and maneuver safely around the eclectic salvage filling every imaginable spot. Ahlwynn stopped when he reached the platform holding the sink Edward had spotted from the ground.

Ahlwynn said, "This is my favorite level."

Edward asked, "Why?"

Ahlwynn answered, "Because this one has the most different kinds."

Edward, sitting with his back against the tree trunk, looked around. The makeshift floor had narrow slats nailed onto supporting planks. A small wooden box held well worn books—-Robinson

THE MOPSTERS

Crusoe, Treasure Island, some paper back Star Wars—-and flashlights. Other randomly located cubbyholes held unidentifiable objects.

He asked, "Different kinds?"

Ahlwynn said, "Whenever I climb this tree, I tell myself a different story. Some of the levels work better for some stories than other levels. But this level," His chest expanded, his smile widened, as he gazed around him. He patted the floor. "This one works for all of them!"

Edward nodded at the floor. "That's some pretty fancy flooring for a treehouse."

Ahlwynn ran his fingers along the grain of the shiny wood floor. "Yep. It took me and Vinny two whole days to install it. Would you believe someone was just going to throw these boards away? Vinny and I found them in a dumpster not three blocks from here."

Edward looked up at the sheet of corrugated metal weaved between several branches above him. He pointed at it. "Where did you find your roof?"

"From a house that burned down."

"The sink?"

"The same house."

Edward stared at the sink. He had to ask. "Why is it sideways?"

For the first time, Ahlwynn looked disappointed.

Edward spoke quickly, "It obviously isn't a sink, not up here. What is it in your stories?"

Ahlwynn's smile returned.

He reached into a cubbyhole and pulled out an old fashion peashooter. In one breath, without a pause, he said, "Say you're stranded on an island in the middle of the Amazon river and angry Yanamani are attacking the fort you had built when you were first stranded, and they were going to try to shoot you with their poison frog darts and you wanted to shoot back, but didn't want to get hit while shooting."

He pulled out a small pouch, poured several pebbles into his hand. He leaned towards the sink. One after another, he used the peashooter to blow the pebbles through the sink's drain hole. "See? I'm protected, they can't get me!"

Ahlwynn carefully returned the peashooter and bag to their cubbyhole. "Or say you're on the Millennium Falcon, and you're out of power, and storm troopers are approaching." He grabbed a flashlight with a red laser. A beam went straight through the drain. A bright red circle appeared on a leaf. "Disintegration!"

Ahlwynn replaced the light to its place. "Or, you think there's bad guys and you want to watch without being seen." He pushed on a slat; it came up, revealing a hidden compartment. Ahlwynn reached in and pulled out a crudely assembled set of small mirrors and wires. He wiggled them through the drain opening. "Perfect!"

The mirrors' small circles, tiny ovals, thin rectangles revealed hidden sights. Edward nodded. "Perfect. Where did you get such a variety of mirrors?"

"Make-up kits. You wouldn't believe how many ladies throw away perfectly good mirrors just because the make-up is gone."

Edward asked, "Ladies give you their old kits?"

Ahlwynn shook his head no. "Naw, we find them in dumpsters."

"We? Your mom goes dumpster diving with you?"

Ahlwynn giggled. "She hates it. Vinny and I do salvage explorations when he's watching me." He looked around, went to a whisper. "Mom has a rule. Anything not used within twenty four hours gets dumped." He double checked his view of the back door. "Sometimes Vinny and I need more time to figure out how to use something. Then I just re-arrange and tell Mom its new stuff."

"Who's Vinny?"

"Mom's cousin. He's fun."

Edward, picking up Treasure Island, said, "My sister says most kids don't read these classics anymore."

THE MOPSTERS

Ahlwynn's smile faded. "The other books were salvage. Not that one."

Edward opened the book. He read out loud the message someone had written on the flyleaf, "Adventure begins when you leave home." He asked, "Where did this one come from?"

Ahlwynn said, "It was my father's, from when he was a kid. He wrote that."

Edward carefully re-secured the book within its protective wooden case. He looked around some more. He saw a long, small diameter metal tube with bright paint decorating almost every inch. Pointing, he asked, "What does that represent?"

For a brief moment Ahlwynn quit smiling. He said, "That is a warrior blowgun." Grabbing his bag of pebbles, he selected one nearly as large of the pipe's opening. "See that leaf over there?"

Edward looked in the direction Ahlwynn pointed. It was full of leaves. He said, "Yes."

Ahlwynn said, "Watch." He puffed on the 'warrior blowgun.'

A leaf shredded. Edward said, "Wow."

Ahlwynn wondered if he dare tell Edward about the special ammo he and Vinny had made for the warrior blowgun, the steel darts that could penetrate plywood. *If shredding a leaf impressed Edward, splicing the branch it grew on would really wow him.* But Ahlwynn had promised Vinny to tell absolutely no one. *A promise is a promise.*

Ahlwynn slid the pipe back to its special holding branches. He looked up. "Want to go higher?" Without waiting for an answer, Ahlwynn climbed higher.

Edward, surprised Ahlwynn didn't want to continue showing off his warrior weapon, followed. He was careful to grab only larger branches and keep close to the trunk. The succeeding levels contained much salvaged 'treasure' most mothers would not have waited even twenty four hours to declare garbage. Seeing the ways Ahlwynn reinvented trash into story props made Edward feel like a boy all over again.

Higher up, almost-musical mobiles and miniature treehouses replaced platforms for people.

The tree trunk swayed. "Ahlwynn, I think this is as high as I dare go."

Ahlwynn shouted down to him, "That's as high as Vinny goes, too."

"You put together everything from here up by yourself?"

"Yup!"

"From dumpster salvage?"

"Yup!"

Clanging noise from down below overpowered Ahlwynn's musical mobiles.

Ahlwynn cried, "Dinner bell!"

Both climbed down.

Just as he stood on the lowest platform, Edward noticed a heart carved into the trunk with the initials

"A H + E B"

in the center. "Ahlwynn, do you have a girl friend?"

Ahlwynn stopped climbing down. He reached over, traced the indented letters with his fingers. "Those were carved before Mom married my father."

He traced the heart outline. "Mom said she got really mad when he did it, telling him, 'You don't deface other people's trees!' He said, 'Don't worry. It will be our tree if you marry me.' Mom said they went right out and made a down payment on the house. Auntie Kaye once told me they did something else right in this tree. I asked Auntie what, and Mom got mad and wouldn't let her answer."

Ahlwynn stared at the heart. "Sometimes it seems every tree branch is an arm and the whole tree is my father hugging me." He skipped the last two branches and leaped to the ground. "Pretty dumb, huh?"

THE MOPSTERS

Edward stepped off the lowest platform. "What happened to your father?"

"He and my mom's parents were killed by a drunk driver the night I was born."

Edward reached up, stroked one of the branches. "You're right about this tree."

Ahlwynn looked up at him. "I'm not a kid. I know what's pretend."

Edward looked down. "I'm not a kid either. There is nothing pretend about your father's love."

Edward followed Ahlwynn into the tiny kitchen area. He marveled a second time how so compact a space could be an effective kitchen. He noticed a table setting was at each end, and the other two plates were set next to each other on the third side, leaving the cramped fourth side free for the cook to maneuver between the stove and table. An elaborate green salad adorned each plate.

Elaine laughed when she saw Edward. His bright yellow polo shirt was no longer spotless and his hands were as grimy as her son's. "I was going to tell my son to wash up for dinner, but I think both of you better."

Edward followed Ahlwynn's lead. Both squeezed passed the chair at the head of the table to scrub their hands at the kitchen sink.

Ahlwynn said, "Wow! I didn't know salad could look so pretty!"

Elaine said, "It's our usual salad, just arranged on plates."

Looking at the bright strips of red peppers, tiny tomatoes and the many fancy sliced vegetables he couldn't identify, Ahlwynn whispered to Edward, "No it's not!"

Edward started to sit at the narrow end across from Ahlwynn. Kaye stopped him, saying "You don't want to be squeezed between the table and the sink." When Edward protested he didn't mind sitting at the sink end, Kaye added, "Elaine likes sitting closer to the sink and stove. It's more convenient." Kaye directed Edward to sit at the long side, the side set with two plates.

Kaye sat down next to Edward. Even sitting as far apart as possible, their arms brushed against each other. She said, "I hope you like tonight's dinner. It's from a recipe our great-grandmother brought over from Italy." She leaned closer to him and stage-whispered, "She said this food made the women in our family the most desirable in the village."

Edward asked, "Salad?"

Elaine, smiling broadly, said, "No, this." She put a large, covered pot onto the table's center. "Our family's secret recipe!" She lifted the lid. Aromatic spices filled the air.

Edward inhaled deeply. "I haven't smelled food that good in years. I bet the aroma alone drove men from all over Italy to your great grandmother's kitchen."

Kaye whispered into Edward's ear. "You should see the pictures of Great-Grandmamma. More than her cooking drove men wild!"

Elaine pulled two half-full bottles from the fridge. "Which salad dressing?"

Kaye, leaning over, whispered so softly into Edward's ear only he heard, "I prefer undressing."

Edward, reddening, spoke loudly, "These veggies look so fresh, I think I'll eat my salad plain."

Ahlwynn, about to grab one of the bottles, pulled his hand back. "I'll have my mine plain, too."

Both sisters suddenly wanted plain salads as well. Elaine returned both bottles to the fridge. The salads were quickly eaten. Elaine proudly spooned large portions of her Italian masterpiece pasta onto each plate.

Edward took a bite. He closed his eyes, a dreamy smile on his face. "Tastes even better than it smells. You could make a living cooking."

Kaye said, "Speaking of making a living, your consulting business sounds exciting. Tell me more."

Edward said, "I can't really tell you much because I sign nondisclosure agreements with all my clients."

Ahlwynn asked, "What's a nondisclosure agreement?"

THE MOPSTERS

Edward explained, "That's a legal term meaning that they will be sharing secrets with me, and I'm not allowed to share those secrets with anyone. Just to make sure I don't accidentally spill the beans, they say I can't say anything. Some companies won't even allow me to say I ever worked with them."

Elaine frowned. "I thought word-of mouth was the best advertising you could get. How can you get recommendations if no one will admit working with you?"

Ahlwynn said, "I bet you have secret codes, like spies!"

Edward blinked. "Very clever. And very close to the truth. I belong to an organization of consultants. My clients' CEOs put in basic information about the type of service I performed, their willingness to use me again and what they did and did not like about my service. I'm given rankings. I submit those files to clients. It is all very hush-hush."

Ahlwynn asked, "What's a CEO?"

Edward said, "A chief Executive Officer, the guy responsible for running the company. Like your Mom is the CEO of The Mopsters." He took a second helping of pasta. "There are flavor combinations in this I've never had before. What are your secret ingredients?"

Elaine started to answer but Kaye interrupted. "Great-Grandpapa didn't get to find out until after their third child was born. Women in our family don't need nondisclosure agreements to keep a secret." She smiled. "Especially secrets worth keeping." She rubbed her now shoeless foot against Edward's leg.

Edward turned to Elaine, "Speaking of trade secrets, what is the secret of your success?"

Elaine replied, "Success?"

Edward said, "You must be successful to consider sending Ahlwynn to my sister's school."

Elaine felt a fear tingle. She thought, *I didn't even know about that school until I raided a client's garbage.* "Uh,"

Kaye interrupted. "My sister's real success is raising a genius son. We like your sister's school, but are not totally convinced it will be challenging enough for Ahlwynn."

Ahlwynn stopped smiling. "You said I was going. You're signing me up Monday!"

Kaye said, "Ahlwynn, how many private schools have we checked out?"

Ahlwynn said, "One."

Kaye said, "Your mom and I were talking. We really like that school, but we owe it to you to check out more than one school."

The rest of the dinner, Edward talked about how his sister's school was easily the best choice.

Elaine felt like she had dodged a bullet. *He should guess from our home I haven't much money. Should I mention my new high paying client, Mr. Strange?* She had a vague feeling that would be a bad idea. *Why?* Suddenly the conversation took a different turn. She heard her sister say,

"Edward, that's a great idea."

Elaine wondered, *what great idea?*

Kaye continued. "Elaine will want to stay here with her son, but as soon as I finish helping Elaine clean up from dinner, we can check out that new pub and enjoy a nightcap."

Elaine, bewildered, wondered what they were talking about. Edward was mumbling something. Everyone had clearly finished eating. Kaye and Ahlwynn were clearing plates. Edward stood. He looked lost. Elaine said, "There isn't that much to clean up. Ahlwynn and I can handle it."

Kaye grinned. "Thanks, Sis." She turned to Edward. "I'll be just a second. Just got to freshen up a bit." Kaye dashed to her room.

Edward stood there, looking first at Kaye's retreating back than at Elaine. "Um, I uh, I mean..."

THE MOPSTERS

Elaine said, "I know what you're going to say. You want to help with dishes. There really isn't much to do. Go have fun."

Edward said, "No, uh,"

Kaye came out of her room. Her skintight, low-cut, sparkle-covered, thigh-high dress showed off her petite body all the ways it was meant to. She grabbed Edward's arm, "Sis will get angry if you argue with her."

Kaye shook her head; her hair flipped. "Let's go!" She led him out the door.

Edward followed like a dog on a leash. He glanced back at Elaine, but she was concentrating on kitchen cleaning and never noticed.

Episode 6: Men, Women and Dragons Who Roar

Ahlwynn, drying a plate, "Looks like Auntie has a new boyfriend."

Elaine concentrated on the large pot, scrubbing the last vestiges of dinner from its well worn interior. Without looking up she said, "One date does not a boyfriend make."

Ahlwynn, grabbing the next plate, said, "But Auntie said—-"

Elaine, scrubbing the now shiny pot even harder, interrupted her son. "Auntie knows a lot about collecting boyfriends," saying boy with a tonality Ahlwynn had not heard before, "But she knows precious little about real men."

Ahlwynn looked up at his mom. "What's the—-"

His Mom cut in again. "Like Kaye said, we should checkout other schools. That much money, we better be sure."

Ahlwynn said, "Mom, that school made me feel normal. I could just be me and be normal. I don't care about the rest of it."

He looked up at his mom, almost on the edge of tears. "Mom, is it wrong to want to be like everybody else, not feel like a freak?"

Elaine looked down at her son. She forgot about the large pot she still held. Thoughts of her sister's flirty ways faded to the far recesses of her mind. "No, honey, it's not wrong. You are normal. You are the kind of normal everyone should be."

Ahlwynn said, "Ms. Charley didn't think so."

Elaine rubbed the steel scrubber against the now spotless pot, pushing harder than when cooked-on food still clung to its sides. "Ms. Charley is an idiot. A zombie making idiot!"

Ahlwynn's eyes widened. "Mom!"

Elaine rinsed off the large pot and slammed it into dish rack. "Ms. Charley is an idiot. She has no right making wonderful boys feel like they aren't normal."

She squatted down, looked directly into her son's eyes. Clutching Ahlwynn's arms, she said, "Ahlwynn, when Kaye said we will be checking out other schools, she lied. I don't have the money. With time, with your help, I think we will, but not right now."

Ahlwynn hugged his mom. "That's OK, Mom. Vinny said I don't need no school. He can teach me the ways of the world just fine."

Elaine hugged him back. "Oh, Ahlwynn, if only that were true." *Why can't I give my son what he needs?*

Elaine's thoughts filled with demanding people getting what they wanted. Ms. Charley demanding easy students. Mr. Strange demanding results. Her sister demanding male attention. *Why can't I—*

"Mom, you're hugging me too tight!"

An hour later Ahlwynn was in bed and hopefully asleep. Elaine went to her room. She softly closed the door, just in case he wasn't asleep.

Kaye has always gone after what, and who, she wants while I sit timidly in shadows. If I'm going to help my son, I have to get out of those shadows and demand my place in the sun! Even thinking to herself, Elaine didn't allow the next words to form in her mind. *A place in the sun, daring to love again.* Images filled her thoughts. *Sun...bright yellow... Edward leaning against his car, the short sleeves of his bright yellow polo shirt straining against his biceps...*

Elaine looked at her reflection in the old dresser mirror. She picked up her cell phone. Put it back down. Elaine, speaking to her reflection, said, "My son is not a freak."

THE MOPSTERS

Tears filled her eyes. She started to reach for the Kleenex box. "No, not tonight." She stared at herself, stood straighter. "Whatever it takes, Ahlwynn will get his chance."

Her tears stopped.

Elaine picked up the phone again; she dialed Vinny's number.

"Hello, Vinny. Free to talk?"

"Make it fast. Got a food pick up, one minute." Elaine knew that meant Vinny was in the restaurant alley, escaping the restaurant kitchen heat, while the chef put finishing touches on a client's meal.

"Vinny, you tell Mr. Strange he knows our work. He himself said it was better than his regular service. Tell him if he wants us on a moment's notice he must pay us a retainer fee, just like other professionals. With a weekly retainer fee, I can drop most of my clients, be ready to clean up after his wild family any time he wants. No retainer, I might not be available next time he calls."

Vinny's voice cracked, "'Laney, people don't tell him terms!"

Elaine took a deep breath. *Is this really me talking?* "That's not all. That work he wants done, it's like two, three days work in one day. Tell him I need more."

Vinny's voice went higher pitch and softer at the same time. "'Laney, you's my favorite cousin. You're family. You're the sister I always wanted. 'Laney, what you're asking for, it ain't healthy."

Elaine said, "What ain't healthy is what Ms. Charley wants done to my son. What ain't healthy is Ahlwynn being told bright and creative isn't normal. You see Mr. Strange, give him my message."

Vinny's voice went soft. "Ahlwynn's crazy about that fancy-schmancy school."

Elaine said, "That school takes fancy-schmancy money. Their best scholarship covers only half the tuition."

Vinny interrupted, "Order's up! Gotta go!"

Elaine hit 'end call.' She knew Vinny would call her back his next break.

F. E. TABOR AND FRAN TABOR

Shaking, Elaine sat down on her bed. *Have I guaranteed my son will go to the school he wants, or have I chased away the only decently paying client I've ever had? Will Vinny talk to Mr. Strange? Will Kaye be mad at me for taking such a chance?*

Elaine decided she didn't care.

~~~

ELAINE SAT AT THE KITCHEN table, an open book in front of her; her eyes on the kitchen wall clock. The clock's hour hand almost touched the twelve. The minute hand jerked upwards, approaching the hour hand. *Almost midnight, Kaye won't be home for at least an hour, maybe not till morning.*

A car door slammed. Startled, Elaine stood up to peer out the kitchen window. She saw Edward's car, and her sister walking towards the back door, her head down. Elaine sat down, resumed staring at her book, as Kaye opened the door. Kaye turned towards the car and waved. Elaine could hear Edward's car drive off.

Elaine said, "You're back early."

Kaye, kicking her shoes off, said, "Edward has a client he has to meet early. Not that it would make much difference. There was a great band at The Balario's. We had danced just enough to reveal Edward knows how to move, when his phone buzzed. 'Business,' he said.

Kaye humphed. "Right. Every call he had to go out to his car, to 'get away from the noise.' It was plenty quiet just outside the entrance. His car was way on the other side of the lot. He just didn't want me to hear. Once, even twice can be business. That much secrecy, it's monkey business! After the tenth exit in as many minutes, I told him to take me home. He looked so relieved it's disgusting!"

Elaine said, "It wasn't his idea to go out tonight, it was yours. Remember he told us how secretive his clients are."

Kaye, unzipping her dress as she headed for her room, shouted back to her sister, "Think about it, 'Laney, what better job for a two-timing

THE MOPSTERS

weasel." Affecting an exaggerated whine, Kaye said, "Sorry, honey, I have to work somewhere, with someone." She popped into her room and emerged seconds later in a nightie. "Sis, why am I always attracted to bad-news-guys?"

Elaine, feeling an irrational urge to defend a man she hardly knew, said, "Kaye, when was the last time one of your bad news guys offered to help with the dishes or chop onions?"

Kaye said, "He didn't actually do those things."

Elaine said, "Any doubts he would have, if we had let him?"

Kaye, heating a cup of milk, shook her head. "No, no doubt at all." She frowned slightly. "I did sort of Shanghai him."

Elaine snorted, "Sort of?"

Kaye, her milk heated and in a mug, sat down next to her sister. "Maybe I should have asked if he had plans." She sipped the milk. "He sure looked good in that yellow tee-shirt."

Elaine thought, *Yes, sister, he looked very good.* Out loud, she corrected her younger sister. "It was a polo shirt."

Kaye said, "I should give Edward a second chance. But my two-timer radar is on!"

Elaine said, "Speaking of men, I called Vinny."

"Huh?"

Elaine continued, "I asked Vinny to deliver a message to Mr. Strange."

Kaye's confusion grew. "Why?"

Elaine told her sister about the demand for both a weekly retainer and higher pay.

Kaye's eyes went wide; she choked on her warm milk. The choking sent her into a coughing fit. Kaye coughed so hard, milk spluttered out her nose, back into her cup. She stared into the now polluted cup, leaned over and dumped it into the sink. "'Laney, I don't know who Mr. Strange really is, but I do know he is not the kind of person you give demands to! And those big gorillas of his! Remember how they lifted up that heavy garbage container like it was nothing? And how they jump every time Mr. Strange speaks?"

Elaine said, "I remember how one of them gave me the creeps when I was on the ladder. But like you said, Mr. Strange has them under control."

Kaye, her eyes even wider, "Elaine, being under Mr. Strange's control is what makes them dangerous!"

Elaine said, "You have seen too many movies."

Kaye said, "What I have not seen too many of is hundred dollar bills, beautiful multi-toned, hundred dollar bills. The money that got our mortgage current, got the electric company off our back, bought our totes and let us buy yummy groceries. Elaine, we can't afford to upset a man with such nice money!"

Elaine said, "I thought it through. If he says no, we are no worse off than we were before. If he says yes, we can say goodbye to Mrs. Simpson and her conniving forever."

Kaye said, "Mr. Strange was the only real chance we had to get your son into a decent school, and you just threw that away."

Elaine said, "Kaye, random jobs do not a reliable income make. If Mr. Strange's money is to help pay the mortgage and Ahlwynn's tuition, it must be steady." Elaine's voice went louder. "We either stand up, demand what we need, or forever remain in the gutters!"

Kaye started to respond when Elaine's phone rang. Elaine's face paled. "It's Vinny."

Kaye said, "Do you suppose he delivered your message to Mr. Strange?" The phone rang again. "Answer it! On speaker phone!"

Elaine swiped her phone, hit the speaker button. "Hello, Vinny. Must be a busy night."

Vinny said, "Very busy, and your little demand made it busier."

Elaine said, "Busier, how?"

Vinny said, "Luck would have it, my friend, for whom you have done such admirable work, came in to order dinner just minutes after

THE MOPSTERS

you called. I waited until he'd eaten his fill, looked to be in a good mood, and I mentioned to him, casual like, you would like better money for your services. 'Lanes, you would not believe the extent of his reaction. He was angry, and weird looking. He got on the phone. Minutes later about a half dozen of his friends, and a couple people I thought he hated were all at his table. They were talking low, but fast and heavy. Anyone got too close, they shut up. Not seen anything like it in months."

Vinny paused. The sisters could hear a muffled conversation. "Another waiter just told me I'm wanted at *the* table. It has something to do with you. I'll call you back soon's I know more." Vinny hung up.

Kaye, her eyes wide, "Sis, this doesn't sound good. I'm scared."

Elaine nodded. "Me, too."

A moment later, the phone rang again, Vinny's number. "Hello, this Elaine?" It was not Vinny's voice.

Elaine, pushing the speaker button, "Yes, this is Elaine."

The voice continued, "Our family has made use of your services a couple times. Your cousin insisted you are reliable. We trusted him. Now we hear you are making demands. What makes you think you can make demands?"

Elaine stifled the urge to squeak 'nothing'. She took a deep breath. Without taking another breath, she spoke in a rapid staccato of words. "My business has many regular clients. Some of those clients are flexible, if I can't make it one day, they don't care if I come another day. Other clients are not so accommodating. I must be there on schedule, or they will not have us come back. Those clients pay less than you, but are reliable every week, all year. Both times you called me were on days I had only the easy going clients. If I had one of the rigid ones, I would not have been able to work for you. I would have been poorer, and you would have been without an emergency clean up crew. Bad for both of us."

Quick intake of air.

Elaine continued. "If I had a weekly retainer, I could afford to drop the rigid clients, keep only the flexible ones and be available to you whenever you need me."

Second quick breath. "But that leaves another problem. I need more supplies for your cleaning jobs than I normally do for a dozen jobs. This means I need more money. The man who paid us said we are the best. The best is worth paying for."

Silence.

Elaine and Kaye heard mumbling.

The unknown man said, "Those your only reasons?"

Elaine and Kaye stared at each other.

Kaye mouthed to her older sister, "Other reasons?"

Elaine shrugged her shoulders. She asked out loud, "Aren't those good reasons?"

"I'll call you back."

The phone went silent.

Elaine and Kaye stared at the silent phone.

It rang.

Elaine answered.

A man said "Hello." It was Mr. Strange. "The homes you have cleaned belong to my family. All expenses are part of a family trust. We decided your requests are reasonable. I know what your highest paying client paid. That will be your retainer. Instead of $1,000 per job, you will get $1,100 per job. Take it or leave it."

Kaye shouted at the speaker phone, "We'll take it!"

Mr. Strange asked, "That your sister?"

Elaine said, "Yes. Raise the retainer by another $50, and we'll take it."

Kaye screamed, "Elaine! Tell the man yes!"

Mr. Strange said, "Listen to your sister. People do not negotiate with me. They take what I offer, or wish they had."

THE MOPSTERS

Elaine said, "The two cleaning jobs I have done for you are the stuff nightmares are made of. If I'm not paid enough, I quit."

The girls heard loud laughter.

Mr. Strange said, "I wish I could hire men with half your guts. Deal."

The phone went silent.

The two sisters stared at each other. Elaine spoke first, barely a whisper, "Do you know what this means?"

Kaye, her largest grin overtaking her face, squealed, "I'll never touch the Simpson cat box again!"

Elaine laughed. "Or clean up after the Simpson brats again!"

Kaye added, "Or have to cook their dinner just to bribe Simpson into paying us what she owes!"

Standing up so fast they knocked their chairs over, the sisters 'high-fived' each other.

They wrapped their arms around each other, jumped up and down and giggled so hard each became dizzy.

Elaine abruptly quit jumping, quit laughing.

She held her sister at arms length. "Kaye, this means I can give my son a fresh start, with new friends at a new school." Elaine's throat tightened. "I can finally give Ahlwynn the chance he deserves."

Suddenly all the tension of the last hours broke loose; all the fears of the last ten years were released; all the tight self-control she had used to hold herself together, all of that and more cascaded out of Elaine in the form of deep, body-shaking sobs. She collapsed onto a still-standing kitchen chair.

Kaye rushed to retrieve the spare roll of bathroom tissue. She handed it to her sister.

Elaine ripped off several squares, blew her nose; a second later needed more squares.

Several minutes later Elaine felt light headed. Most of the new roll of bathroom tissue filled the waste basket. She smiled feebly at her sister. "So many times I cried alone when I thought we were going to be homeless. I shouldn't be crying now."

Kaye, scooting a chair close to her sister, put her arm around her. "Sis, you have had reason to cry ever since," she paused. "Ever since I had to tell you why our parents, why Ahlwynn senior, did not come for your son's birth, would never come. Sure, you've shed a few tears. Some nights, you whimpered into your pillow all night long. But the flood you should have been shedding? That I never once saw you do, not until tonight, until now." She hugged her sister.

Both girls, arms tightly around each other, cried together; crying harder than either had before. They cried for lost childhood, lost dreams, lost hope. They cried for their new dreams, for the reemergence of hope.

Much later that night, finally in bed and about to drift off to sleep, Elaine thought of all the times her sister had been there for her.

Kaye had dropped out of high school to move in with her and Ahlwynn. Kaye had taken turns with her to walk her son those nights he wouldn't stop crying. Kate hired on to the only fast food place within walking distance so she could earn extra cash without the added expense of a second car. Without the pittance Kaye earned flipping burgers, Elaine would have lost her home the same year she lost her husband.

Elaine remembered the enthusiasm Kaye showed when they started their cleaning company. Elaine's final thoughts as she drifted off to sleep, *How can I feel so much jealousy for the best sister anyone ever had, over a man I hardly know? Especially now, when we finally have a chance?*

But deep inside, Elaine knew the ugly nugget of jealousy was real.

Kaye, you asked for the return of 'Dragon Lady.' Tonight, talking to Mr. Strange, I was Dragon Woman. When next we see Edward, watch out! This Dragon Woman gets what she wants!

Episode 7: Gimmicks!

The next morning Vinny showed up for breakfast, envelope in hand. "The family said in the future, all retainer funds will be paid on Monday, but they wanted you to have this first one early as a show of good faith."

Ahlwynn asked, "Vinny, why is Mr. Strange paying my mom when she hasn't done any more cleaning?"

Vinny explained, "It's so she doesn't need other clients. She is taking money to be available whenever he calls, at a moment's notice. Plus when she does clean, she will get more."

Ahlwynn said, "Mom, you should be available to clean for everyone in town. You would make so much money just being available; you would never have to work again!"

All three adults burst into laughter.

After breakfast Elaine called Ms. Simpson. The phone call was short and sweet. "...No, not even then. I'm sorry, we have so much work, we just don't have time...I said, we are quitting...Bye." Elaine hung up while Ms. Simpson still protested. Vinny, Kaye and Ahlwynn burst into giggles.

Kaye said, "That's a turn around from what she has always said before." Holding her nose up as snotty as she could, Kaye mimicked Ms. Simpson. "I don't know why I pay you anything, you are the worst!" Kaye changed facial expressions to desperate pleading. "Please, please, please keep cleaning for me! You are the best!"

Everyone giggled even harder. Elaine sang, "No more Simpson cat box!"

Vinny said, "Laney, I always told ya, you's too meek and mild. You should have demanded respect from that woman the first day you worked for her."

Elaine stopped smiling. "Vinny, for the first time, I think you are right."

The following Monday, Elaine and Ahlwynn went to the new school to formally fill out the scholarship application. They were assured Ahlwynn qualified for their best scholarship and a reduced deposit.

When Elaine explained it would be two weeks before she had even the reduced sign up funds, Kathy suggested Ahlwynn be a visitor those weeks. Elaine would have said no, but her son's eyes lit up so much at the prospect, she relented.

Kathy smiled down at Ahlwynn. "If your mother has no objections, how about your visiting start right now?"

Ahlwynn looked over at his mother. "Can I?"

Elaine nodded yes.

Kathy said, "I'll walk with you to the classroom and explain to my assistant you will be visiting the next few weeks. When your paperwork catches up, you will be formerly enrolled." She turned to Elaine. "When I come back, we will finish the scholarship application together."

AN HOUR LATER, ELAINE and Kaye sat drinking coffee together at their kitchen table.

Elaine said, "Ahlwynn looked so happy when I left. It was nice of Kathy to let him be a 'visitor' until we earn the full deposit." Elaine took a sip. "Was she so generous on her own? Or did her brother ask her to be nice?"

Kaye said, "Elaine, who cares? I doubt her brother can force Kathy to take every kid off the street. Now we can tell both the authorities and

THE MOPSTERS

Mrs. Green the truth, Ahlwynn is in school." Kaye smiled at her sister. "Not working today, I feel like a kid ditching school."

Elaine frowned. "Me, too. The one and only time I skipped school, I felt guilty for a week. It was miserable!"

Kaye shook her head. "Laney, Laney, Laney. The skipping feeling is a fun feeling!" She sighed. "If it makes you feel better, pretend like you are looking at the Simpson cat box, filled with a full week's worth of cat do-do."

Elaine, remembering the sight and smell of the overfull cat box, squinched her nose.

Kaye continued, "Now imagine you are taking that box, and dumping it upside down in the middle of Mrs. Simpson's kitchen floor."

Elaine's eye's widened. "How could you!" Abruptly Elaine remembered Vinny's admonition, 'You should have demanded respect from that woman.' *Would threatening Mrs. Simpson with that neglected cat box have made her respect me? Goodness knows, every time she griped I wasn't fast enough, I wanted to just toss it at her.* Elaine visualized Mrs. Simpson cringing as cat box litter rolled across the floor. Elaine couldn't help smiling.

Kaye sat up straighter. "Now you're getting it! Playing hooky is fun!"

Elaine smiled. "I'm looking forward to the rest of the week. The clients we kept are such pleasant people."

Kaye rolled her eyes. "You're hopeless, Elaine. You can visit people without working for them."

Kaye's eyes lit up. "Elaine, we have the day off. We can do anything. I'm going to call Edward and see if he's free for lunch." As she spoke, Kaye pulled out her phone and punched Edward's number.

Elaine's good mood evaporated.

Kaye, oblivious to her sister's changed attitude, frowned at her phone. "Straight to voice mail."

On the beep, Kaye said "Hi, Kaye here. If you're free for lunch, call."

Elaine snapped, "Don't pester people during work hours!"

Kaye said, "Pestering?"

Elaine, in a rapid rush, yelled, "Pestering! You meet a nice man! Next thing, you hone in on him like a mosquito, smother him like a wet blanket, then drown him in so much attention the good guys run away but bad guys lap it up, sucking the lifeblood out of you!"

Kaye stared at her sister. "Sis, first you challenge Mr. Strange, then you tackle Mrs. Simpson. Now you are yelling nonsense at me for no reason. What is wrong with you?"

Elaine slammed her cup on the table. Coffee splashed out. "Nothing is wrong with me. We needed more money. Mrs. Simpson needed to be told unequivocally no, we are never going to work for her again. You, baby sister, need to be told to back off; don't chase away the good ones."

Kaye stared at Elaine's spilled coffee. Eyes wide, she stared at her sister's anger-contorted face. "Elaine, I wanted my Dragon Lady Sister back, but you're being Dragon Bitch! What is going on?"

Elaine snapped, "Going on? I've given you advice before."

Kaye said, "Not like this. Not yelling. Especially not about a lunch. Laney, what's wrong?"

Elaine's thoughts whirled. *What's wrong? I can't stop thinking about Edward. Why didn't I think about asking him for lunch? If he's busy, or just claims to be busy, no big deal. It's just lunch. I didn't think of it because unlike you, dear sister, I am out of practice. I haven't tried to get any man's attention since, since...* Even in her thoughts Elaine couldn't finish the sentence. *Why can't I be more like you?*

Acting like she had just noticed her spilled coffee, Elaine reached over to the sink and grabbed the damp dishrag. Wiping up her mess, Elaine said, "Sorry. It's just that, now everything is working out. Ahlwynn is in a good school. The bank won't repo our home. Heck, you might finally have a decent boyfriend. Everything seems so perfect. Sis, last time I felt this good, the doctor told me I had a beautiful baby

THE MOPSTERS

boy. I couldn't wait for, for" She took a quick breath, skipped saying the name. "To show up with our parents, to show off the beautiful child we had created. Instead, the next person in the room was you, telling me they will never come. Sis, feeling this good scares me."

While speaking, Elaine discovered she was telling her sister the truth. *No wonder I didn't think of calling Edward. I'm terrified of happiness.*

Kaye said, "Oh, Elaine—-"

Kaye's phone beeped. Text message. "Can't today. Tomorrow noon? Text back, in a meeting."

Kaye hit the icon to text back. "Working rest of week. Dinner again?"

Return text, "Not free until Sunday. If I brought food, would you girls let me cook it?"

"Yes."

"It's a date. See you one o'clock Sunday."

Both sisters felt their hearts flutter.

Only Kaye smiled.

The rest of the week went as anticipated. Ahlwynn loved his new school more each day. Cleaning for only their most easy going clients was almost fun. Mrs. Green gave the girls one of her brother's old high school math books because, "Unlike those other books, math doesn't go out of date." Her parting words to them, "Please bring Ahlwynn back when school is not in session."

When they gave the book to Ahlwynn he grinned. "A grown up book! I can't wait to bring it to school to show Tim!"

"Tim?"

Ahlwynn said, "You remember, the boy who showed us around at the open house?"

Elaine said, "I remember him. He seemed nice."

Ahlwynn said, "Mom, he's not just nice, he's cool. He does things with the school robot the big kids have trouble matching."

Ahlwynn grinned broadly, "And he's my best friend." He flopped down on their couch, already checking out the 'grown up' math book. "Tell me when dinner's ready."

Her son's eagerness to share a 'grown up' math book made Elaine remember a night just a few months earlier. Ahlwynn had been unusually quiet at dinner, barely picked at his food. When asked, 'What's wrong?' he mumbled 'Nothing.'

The next day at breakfast Ahlwynn had asked her what was so wrong with being excited about library time. Elaine later learned boys teased him about loving books. *Now my son is free to enjoy books with friends!* Ahlwynn's current happiness revealed just how miserable he had been at his old school.

Strength welled up within Elaine. *Whatever it takes, you will stay in Kathy's School.*

Saturday arrived.

Ahlwynn woke to the sound of the vacuum cleaner. He looked at his wall clock. Not even seven! *Mom must be vacuuming. Any minute now, Auntie will be yelling 'Saturday sleep-in time is sacred!'* Rubbing sleep from his eyes, Ahlwynn opened his door, and stared in shock. Auntie Kaye rapidly pushed the vacuum back and forth over their 'living room' carpet. His aunt smiled at him as he stumbled his way to the bathroom, where he saw his mother on her hands and knees cleaning the floor. Ahlwynn mumbled "Huh?"

His mom looked up. "Need to use the facilities?" Assuming a yes, she got up. Ahlwynn asked, "Mom, what are you doing?"

Elaine answered, "When I heard Kaye turn on the vacuum, I decided it was the perfect time to clean the bathroom. Don't take too long. I've lots left to do in here. Make yourself some cold cereal."

Ahlwynn protested, "Mom, it's Saturday! Pancake day!"

"No time. After you've eaten, start cleaning your room."

THE MOPSTERS

An hour later, Vinny stopped by for pancakes. The sisters told him he could, like Ahlwynn, have cold cereal. After the cold cereal, he and Ahlwynn attempted to escape outside.

Kaye said, "There's garden tools in the garage. Why don't the two of you start weeding?"

Ahlwynn's face dropped.

Vinny protested, "I promised Ahlwynn—-"

Kaye interrupted, "You've been promising to show Ahlwynn manly skills like yard work for years. Today is your lucky day!"

Vinny said, "Then we'll need manly levels of food."

Kaye said, "Pancakes, all you can eat, for lunch."

Ahlwynn rushed out the door. Even weeding beat cleaning his already clean room. Vinny followed him out the door.

VINNY HALF HELD HIS breath as he opened the garage side door and flipped the switch. The single dangling light bulb casted yellow-hued light into the windowless interior. Most modern sheds had more room than the dirt-floored garage. Built for the cars of the early 1900's, even if the garage's junk-filled interior were miraculously emptied, few modern vehicles could have squeezed into it.

The garage smelled acrid and felt like a defunct museum. A spider web covered, mechanical reel lawn mower leaned against a short wooden shelf. Oily dust covered the shelf so thickly everything stored on it blended into the shelf's surface. Several hand spades lay on the dirt floor.

Stacks of old boxes lined all four walls, even the barn-style opening once meant for cars. Wooden crates with peeling labels filled the bottom rows. Layers of sagging, grimy cardboard boxes squatted above the crates.

In sharp contrast, the uppermost layer held boxes with rigid, straight edges framing smooth, honey-colored, flat sides. Vinny remembered adding those new-looking boxes to the ancient stacks. He and Kaye had rushed through her parent's apartment, struggling to salvage every memory-filled piece of clothing, jewelry, bric-a-brac, albums, toiletries and anything else they could grab and cram into those boxes. They had stuffed the last box just minutes ahead of the landlord's eviction squad.

Ahlwynn held his nose. "It stinks in here."

Vinny said, "That stink is why we store our alley-salvage outside the garage, not in it!" He glanced at the hand spades, then the lawn mower. "Ahlwynn, what do you think is more important, a few weeds, or all the grass in your front yard?"

Ahlwynn said, "The grass, but—"

Vinny interrupted, "Don't you think it's about time your mom stopped relying on her neighbor's generous lawn mowing?"

Ahlwynn said, "He likes showing off his riding lawn mower."

Vinny said, "But if someone were to rebuild that fine piece of machinery..."

Ahlwynn now understood where Vinny's line of questioning was heading. "Then I could mow the grass. Much more important than weeding."

Vinny grabbed the old reel mower and pulled it out into the sunlight, the first sunlight it had seen in over a half century. "Our first order of business is cleaning this enough to start working on it." He thumped it against the ground. Dust flew, mystery chunks fell to the ground; spiders ran up the handle. Vinny brushed them off. "I spotted a couple old metal files on the shelf and an oil can. I've tools in my car. Think we can bring this thing back to life?"

Ahlwynn said, "Yes!" He loved 'mechanic-ing' with cousin Vinny even more than he hated weeding. With luck, the dilapidated lawn mower could take days to fix.

Vinny said, "Get the garden hose. First step, a lawn mower shower!"

THE MOPSTERS

Two hours later, lawn mower pieces lay scattered across an old tarp, each section as clean as the day it was made, and nearly as devoid of paint. It had taken the two of them together to budge screws and bolts rusted together.

Vinny held one of the metal files found in the garage. As he expected, it was just the right hardness and grit to sharpen the blade. The second file was similar, but a finer grit. Vinny explained to Ahlwynn, "When this was built, people needed things to last a long time. See how thick the cutting blades are? They are meant to be hand-sharpened thousands of times. The man who bought this mower didn't just buy it for himself. He expected his sons and their sons in turn to use it."

Ahlwynn asked, "What about daughters and granddaughters?"

Vinny said, "Lawn mowers like this take he-man muscles. Even butter-churning, rug-beating lady pioneers had trouble working one of these. That's part of the reason your great-great grandparents had men's work and woman's work."

Ahlwynn said, "My mom doesn't like being told she can't do man's work."

Vinny said, "Women like your mom are the reason things changed." Vinny winked. "Officially." He handed Ahlwynn a file. "Show me how you would sharpen that blade."

Ahlwynn rubbed the file along the blade's edge. He could feel the vibration of the rough file scraping against the pitted lawn mower blade. A few red-brown flakes of rust drifted downward. Ahlwynn scowled. "This will take forever!"

Vinny said. "Ease up a bit; try a smaller angle." To illustrate what he meant, Vinny held the other file against the cutting edge, slanting closer to the main curve. "Think knife edge. The blade must slice into the grass like a very sharp knife slicing paper."

Matching his cousin's angle, Ahlwynn worked his file against the old blade. Bright new metal started to peak out from the tarnished surface. The curve on the twisted blade made it difficult to maintain the correct angle, but Ahlwynn persevered.

When he spotted the first bit of bright metal start to peak out from the dull rust, he focused even more intently on the full curve of the old blade.

His hands soon developed a rhythm of their own. Slide, push, over, back…slide, push, over, back… Ahlwynn worked the file, transforming 'dead' rust into useful blade. He became oblivious to all else, except for the sound of metal scraping metal. The first blade finished, he went on to do the rest.

In his mind he traveled the world, resurrecting lost tools, saving them from ignoble trash heaps.

Vinny watched Ahlwynn closely. Satisfied the boy was doing fine, he lay back on the grass, hands behind his head, gazing at the scudding clouds more than his young cousin.

Ahlwynn worked the file over the mower's final blade. His hands stopped feeling the file's vibrations. "My hand tingles funny." He shook his hand to get the numbness out. He ran his finger along the newly shiny surface. "That's pretty knife-edgy."

Vinny sat up. "Lots of folk would settle for that. There were two files." Vinny handed Ahlwynn the second file. "What's different about this file?"

Ahlwynn held it. "It feels lighter, but not much, and the filing part is finer, almost like sandpaper." He frowned. "If I had been using this file, it would have taken hours longer to file those edges."

Vinny said, "The coarse file is designed for big chunks. This will sand off the edge, make it truly razor sharp. When I was your age, I mowed lawns, but we didn't have money for a power mower. I used an old fashion mower a lot like this one. I filed its blades every night that summer." Vinny ran his hand along a blade. "It cut grass so sweet."

Ahlwynn asked, "Didn't using an old fashion mower make it take too long to mow? How could you have made any money?"

THE MOPSTERS

Vinny laughed, "Already thinking like your mother. I made the same complaint to my old man. He said I was looking at it all wrong. It wasn't how many lawns and how fast, it was dollars in my pocket at the end of the day. He claimed what I needed was a gimmick."

Ahlwynn, now carefully using the finishing file, asked, "Gimmick?"

"Gimmick. A reason to get people to pay me more."

Ahlwynn blinked hard, frowned slightly. He looked up at his cousin. "A lawn mowing gimmick?"

Vinny laughed. "My response exactly. He told me to come up with a reason old fashion reel mowers were better than power mowers. He claimed if I came up with a good enough reason, people would pay me more than they did the power mower guys." Vinny noticed Ahlwynn had slowed down. "Keep Filing."

Ahlwynn asked, "The gimmick?"

Vinny said, "A neighbor threw away a stack of gardening magazines. The front cover of one showed a guy pushing an old fashion mower with the big headline, 'Why Push Mowers are Kinder to Grass.' I carried that magazine to every house, showed people the cover and said that's why they had to pay me double what they did those lazy power mower users. I cleaned up that summer."

"How come you didn't keep mowing lawns?"

Vinny leaned closer, whispered, "End of summer, I sold my mower, with the magazine, to a friend." Vinny chuckled. "Truth is, it was too much like work. Learn to use this," Vinny tapped Ahlwynn's head. "You'll need less of this." He tapped Ahlwynn's arm. "Remember, the guy with the best angle, the best gimmick, he's got the edge."

Ahlwynn looked up from his filing. "How come you didn't tell my Mom she should have a cleaning gimmick?"

Vinny said, "Tried to. Your Mom yelled gimmicks are cheating. Kaye got it, but your Mom? She is one stubborn lady."

Elaine's piercing shout interrupted them. "Come and get it!"

The two cousins jumped up, started to run to the house. Vinny stopped, grabbed Ahlwynn's arm. He whispered, "Ahlwynn, best not mention anything about gimmicks to your Mom."

Ahlwynn nodded. "Got it."

Racing ahead of Vinny, Ahlwynn flung the screen door open. "I smell pancakes!"

Vinny chimed in, "and hot maple syrup!"

Elaine and Kaye shouted in unison, "No-o-o-o-o!" They charged the duo, shoving them back into the yard. "No way are you coming in here! You're both filthy!"

Vinny stumbled backwards. "Let us in to wash up."

Elaine said, "We'll bring a pan of soapy water out here. Take your shoes off before you come in."

Ahlwynn and Vinny looked at each other. Sure, they were both dirty from cleaning up the old mower, but many times both of them had come inside far grimier. Ahlwynn asked, "Wouldn't it be easier to let us use the sink?"

Kaye already carried a pot filled with soapy water into the yard. "Easier for you two, maybe, but not for us!" She sat the pot down on the ground.

Elaine reemerged from the house with washcloths and towels. "Remember, shoes off before you come in!"

Ahlwynn and Vinny dutifully washed up and entered the kitchen stocking-footed. Both of them stopped short, looked around; eyes large, mouths open.

Ahlwynn said, "Wow! I didn't know walls could shine!"

Vinny said, "Wow is right." He glanced at the small table. A big stack of hot cakes sat on a plate in its center, a steaming ceramic pitcher of hot syrup next to it. "That looks and smells so good, but I'm half afraid to come in."

THE MOPSTERS

AN HOUR LATER, FULL of pancakes, Vinny leaned back in his chair, ready to enjoy a final cup of coffee.

Elaine, grabbing his cup, said, "Out! Kaye and I are cleaning the kitchen next."

Ahlwynn stared at the spotless cupboards, stove and fridge. "What's left to clean?"

Vinny said, "Ahlwynn, remember how we used two files?"

Ahlwynn nodded.

Vinny said, "They are about to fine-file clean and the smartest thing we men can do is get out while the getting is good."

As they went out the door, Vinny shouted at the sisters, "What's his name?"

Elaine said, "The place needs cleaning."

At the same time Kaye said, "Whose name?"

Ahlwynn rolled his eyes. "Edward. Mom cooked him dinner, now he's coming over tomorrow to cook for us."

Vinny said, "Maybe I should trade shifts, so as to be here tomorrow when this Edward shows up."

Both sisters, eyes fear-wide, shouted, "No-o-o-o!"

Vinny, his hand over his heart, said, "I'm hurt, right here. You think I'll say something uncouth?"

Kaye said, "Think? I know you will. Right after you give him the third degree. Now out!" She tossed a wet wash rag at Vinny's rapidly retreating back. The rag hit the swinging screen door.

Back at the reassembled lawn mower, Vinny slowly worked the freshly oiled gears. "Kaye's had lots of boyfriends. Ever seen her clean like this before?"

Ahlwynn said, "She'd clean house before they came over, but not like this."

Vinny nodded. "Your Mom ever help?"

Ahlwynn said, "No, she always griped about Auntie's boyfriends."

Vinny worked the lawn mower's handle up and down, gave it a test push. "Ahlwynn, what you have in there," He pointed at the house. "Is two women in love with the same man. That house cleaning? It's a gimmick."

"Huh?"

Vinny nodded. "Dollars to doughnuts, he said something about liking a clean house."

Ahlwynn thought hard. "He said something about bachelor living."

Vinny grinned widely. "Yup! Their sudden love of deep housecleaning is one hundred percent gimmick. And Ahlwynn, when they figure out they both want the same boyfriend, be careful. It will be war."

Ahlwynn shook his head. "That's silly. Mom's way too old for boyfriends."

Vinny smiled. "Ahlwynn, she's twenty eight. Only four years older than your Auntie Kaye."

Ahlwynn frowned. He grabbed the lawn mower from Vinny. "Let's see if this thing cuts grass." He shoved the mower hard across the unkempt lawn. Grass bits flew; a path emerged.

The rhythmic sh-sh-sh-sh-sh of the sharpened mower blades slicing grass blended into other warm-weather-soft outdoor sounds.

Vinny started to say something. Ahlwynn shouted, "Can't hear over the mower!"

SUNDAY MORNINGS WERE supposed to be lazy, quiet times. Instead Ahlwynn woke to find his make-shift desk lowered, and his mom standing on it, removing the cover from his dome light. "Mom, what are you doing?"

His mother carefully lowered the glass cover to the desk top, jumped down to the floor and explained, "I don't know how Kaye and I missed the light fixtures! Each and every one is filthy!"

THE MOPSTERS

For the first time, Ahlwynn noticed many dead insects filled the bowl-shaped light cover.

Ahlwynn heard his Aunt Kaye shout, "Don't pour the dead flies into the kitchen waste basket! Dump them into the outside garbage!" Ahlwynn followed his Mom out of the bedroom. Every light fixture cover and most of the light bulbs were lined up on the kitchen table.

An hour later, all light covers and bulbs were now as immaculate as the rest of the little bungalow and back where they belonged.

Ahlwynn started to grab the loaf of bread on the counter. Auntie Kaye shrilled, "What are you doing?"

Ahlwynn looked around, attempting to fathom the problem. He said, "Making toast."

His mom and aunt shouted in unison, "No!" His mom explained, "Toast makes crumbs. We just cleaned the toaster. Have plain bread, with peanut butter. Make it over the sink, just in case."

"In case what?"

Kaye said, "You know what."

Ahlwynn started to protest he did not know what, but Kaye continued talking. "Since it will be a few hours before we eat, I'll make peanut butter sandwiches for all of us."

Ahlwynn started to protest he wanted toast, but one glance at his mom told him to keep silent.

After 'breakfast,' the sisters again cleaned the kitchen. Then both sisters disappeared into their rooms, their last words to Ahlwynn, "Don't touch anything!"

Ahlwynn escaped his hospital-operating-room-sterile home for the warm comfort of his tree. He climbed up to his favorite level. Nestled into a comfortable crook, he grabbed small binoculars from one of his hidden shelves. Searching for nothing in particular, he surveyed the neighborhood. He was high enough to see both of his home's side yards and the front yard of the house across the street. *Gimmick. Cousin Vinny said crazy-level housecleaning is a gimmick; Mom and Kaye think it will make Edward like them better.* The whole idea sounded lame to Ahlwynn, but girls could get funny ideas.

The other thing Vinny said, about his mother wanting a boyfriend, that wasn't just lame. *Vinny's wrong. Mom is a MOM, not some man-chasing fool like Auntie!*

Ahlwynn loved his Auntie Kaye, but felt there was something not right about how a new 'perfect' man seemed to hang around her every week. *If Mom starts acting like Auntie...* The thought made the pit of his stomach tighten. He gripped a smooth tree branch, imagined the father he never knew hugging him. *If Mom becomes more like Auntie, how can she stay a mom?*

Ahlwynn noticed his across-the-street neighbor Mr. Anderson go outdoors with his small dog on a leash. Ahlwynn focused his binoculars on them, imagining the dog's collar held secret documents. On their walk someone will innocently ask Mr. Anderson, 'Can I pet your charming dog?' Only it won't be innocent, charming will be code. When Mr. Anderson says yes, you may pet my charming dog, his fellow spy will think it is safe to kneel down, retrieve the documents from the dog's collar. Only it won't be safe because they are being watched...

Ahlwynn's imagination created more excitement for Anderson's Sunday stroll than James Bond experienced in an entire movie.

Motion in the distance.

Ahlwynn focused his binoculars. Edward's white sedan! Ahlwynn started to climb down, but stopped. Remembering Vinny's words, he decided to watch.

The car turned into Ahlwynn's driveway, parked near the back door. Edward got out, opened the car's back door, pulled out two heavy looking old-fashion paper grocery bags and what looked like a small suitcase. His arms around the grocery bags, gripping the suitcase by the handle, Edward headed for the back door. The door flew open before he was halfway there. Kaye and his Mom rushed out, each grabbed a bag. Telling Edward "Hi", they led him into the house.

THE MOPSTERS

Several minutes passed. Ahlwynn kept expecting his mom to call him, demanding he come in. It didn't happen.

Is Mom going to start being more like Auntie, acting weird whenever a man comes around?

His Auntie too often decided boyfriend time was more important than family time. The tight feeling within Ahlwynn's stomach grew tighter. *Why isn't Mom calling?*

A second mystery occurred to Ahlwynn. *Who brings a suitcase to a dinner?*

Convincing himself the only reason he was going inside was to solve The Suitcase Mystery, Ahlwynn climbed down the tree and sauntered over to the house. About to push open the screen door, he could hear his mom and aunt laughing, telling Edward they had never seen such things.

Through the screen, he could see the open case unfolded on the kitchen table, the three adults crowded around it.

Ahlwynn asked through the screen, "What things?"

Startled, Elaine turned to see her son come in. "Come see what Edward brought."

Her son just stood there, staring at her. Elaine added, "It's stuff he used in college."

Kaye said, "Ed did dinner parties to sell cooking supplies to help pay for college. This is his personal display set he used in those days." She looked up at Edward, smiling and batting her longer-and-darker-than-usual eyelashes at him. "Eddy is practically a gourmet cook."

Ahlwynn still just stood, staring. *Eddy?*

Elaine said, "Edward has equipment I didn't know existed. Come see."

Ahlwynn slowly walked the three steps to the table. Normally he would have been excited about new gadgets, but right now he was more concerned about the strange woman with his mother's voice. He was accustomed to Kaye's make-up transformations and special-date-hairstyling but had never before seen his mother so altered.

He remembered an old movie he had watched with his mom, how she had laughed when a lady in the movie called applying make-up "putting on war paint."

His Mom wore 'war-paint' as powerful as what his aunt wore, and her hair was even fancier. He had no idea his mom owned fancy jeans with shiny glittery things all over them. She looked like one of those fancy ladies in a magazine, perhaps just a bit heavier.

His Mom was beautiful, not just to him, but whole world beautiful.

Not really interested, Ahlwynn pointed to a shiny metal object in the custom-padded case. "What's that?"

Edward said, "That is an attachment that allows me to turn one of these," He picked up a cucumber from the pile of fresh vegetables heaped on the small dinette, tossed it whirling into the air and caught it again. "Into a magical work of art."

Edward took all the gadgets out of their storage slots, closed the now empty case and sent it sliding away on the polished floor. As more items of food were retrieved from the grocery bags, he proceeded to give his audience the cooking show he had been trained to give so many years earlier.

The sisters oohed and awed over every spiral and floret Edward created from his assortment of vegetables. They applauded his rapid meat slicing. They thrilled at his fry pan food-flips. In spite of himself, Ahlwynn became almost as enthralled as his mom and aunt.

It was the best dinner Ahlwynn had ever eaten. *Cousin Vinny was wrong. It's neat having Mom look so pretty. It's nice having the house so clean. This isn't war, it's good.*

After dinner Edward insisted on doing a full kitchen clean up. Ahlwynn watched, amazed neither his aunt nor his mother used being 'dressed up' as an excuse to not help with dishes.

THE MOPSTERS

Both sisters encouraged Edward to stay longer, but he said he had to leave early the next day to fly out of town. Edward suggested he *might* be able to come next Sunday, show them one of the other meals his old employer had taught him. The two sisters kept interrupting each other saying, yes! Come!

As soon as Edward's car left the driveway, Kaye snapped, "Elaine, you kept getting in Eddy's way!"

Elaine said, "I can't believe you call him Eddy! He is clearly the *Edward* type. I was helping. You were shoving your—" Elaine shrugged her shoulders, thrusting her chest out in a way Ahlwynn had seen his aunt do, but never his mother! His mother finished her sentence. "So-called assets into his face. Nice men don't like tramps!"

Kaye shouted back, "Tramps! At least I am dressed nice! Look at you, blouse so unbuttoned, you might as well left it open!"

Elaine, her voice higher pitched than Ahlwynn could recall hearing it, "At least I have a bra on. And those eyelashes! Clowns wear less make up!"

The sisters never noticed Ahlwynn fleeing to his room, or his door slamming. They were too busy slamming their own doors.

The next morning, Ahlwynn noticed his mom and aunt seemed normal, they just didn't talk as much as usual during breakfast or the ride to school.

Episode 8: Sisters forever, or not

After school, Ahlwynn and Tim, Ahlwynn's best friend, waited together for their mothers. As usual, both of their mothers were late. Ahlwynn said, "It was as bad as cousin Vinny warned me it would be. Mom and Auntie have yelled at each other before, but the next morning they laugh and talk like nothing happened. This morning was almost worse than the yelling. They acted so polite, they were rude."

Tim asked, "How can polite be rude?"

Ahlwynn explained, "Say I want to borrow the book you're holding. I'd say, 'Can I borrow the book.' All casual, because we're friends. But if I said, 'Master Tim, if it would not be too much trouble, would you consider lending me the book you are holding. I will, of course, treat it with the utmost care.' And you took just as long to say yes or no, that would be like using all those words to fill up space, like a wall of words."

Tim said, "So your mom and aunt are talking a lot but saying nothing?"

Ahlwynn shook his head. "It is even weirder than that. When they aren't taking forever to say almost nothing, they are silent."

Tim shook his head. "Weird. All because they like the same guy?"

Ahlwynn said. "Yup. The funny thing is, I don't think Edward has a clue both my aunt and my mom like him."

Tim said, "You said your aunt practically forced him to go dancing after that first dinner."

Ahlwynn nodded. "Yes, he knows Auntie likes him, a lot. But I don't think he knows my mom likes him more."

F. E. TABOR AND FRAN TABOR

Two cars drove up into the school's lot.

Ahlwynn exclaimed, "They're here!"

Instead of waiting for Ahlwynn to come to the car, Elaine got out and walked over to the two boys. "Hi, aren't you Tim, the young man who greeted us during the open house?"

Tim nodded yes.

"I would like to ask a favor of your mother. Can I get her phone number and name?"

Tim said, "You can ask her yourself. She's in the car behind you."

Elaine hadn't paid attention to the vehicle parked behind hers. Walking up to it, she stared at the emblem on its nose. *Mercedes makes a van?* Elaine tapped the passenger side window. The car window glided into the door.

Leaning down into the window, Elaine held out her hand. She said, "Hi! I'm Elaine, Ahlwynn's mom. Ahlwynn talks about your son so much."

Tim's mother stared at Elaine's hand a moment before responding. Giving the proffered hand more a quick grasp than a true handshake, she said, "I'm Alice. Tim talks about Ahlwynn, too."

Elaine smiled what she hoped was a super-friendly smile. "Look, I know we just met, but Tim is such a very nice boy, I'm sure you must be just as nice."

Alice's face went neutral. "Uh, thank you." She shouted out her window, "Tim, hurry up."

Tim came running.

Elaine spoke faster. "I'm in a bind. I have an emergency cleaning job Friday. From experience there won't be time to come get Ahlwynn and still finish on time. Could you take Ahlwynn home with you Friday? I can pick him up as soon as I get off work. Please, I don't have anyone else. My sister works with me; my cousin has all day Friday shift. It will only be until seven."

THE MOPSTERS

Before Alice could answer, Tim said, "Mom, Ahlwynn could spend the night!"

Alice opened her mouth, closed it. She looked at her son. "Oh, all right." She looked at Elaine, "Your son might as well stay the night. Will you pick him up by noon?"

Elaine felt her knees go weak with relief. "Noon sharp! Thank you!"

Tim ran back to Ahlwynn. "We're going to have an overnighter! Friday, you're coming home with me and we're having an overnighter!"

ON THE WAY HOME AHLWYNN asked, "Mr. Strange have another cleaning gig for you Friday?"

His mom answered, "Yes, and I'm afraid it might take too long. You notice Kaye isn't with us."

Ahlwynn, hoping his mom wasn't pointing out the obvious for a bad reason, said, "Kaye is often off doing her own thing."

Elaine repeated his last three words. "Her own thing!"

Stop sign ahead, Ahlwynn expected his mom to start slowing down. She didn't.

"Mom!"

Elaine's eyes went wide. She slammed the break pedal.

All four tires squealed.

The car screeched to a halt halfway into the intersection.

A honking car, its tires squealing just as loudly as Elaine's, came rushing from Ahlwynn's side. It careened around their Subaru.

Ahlwynn yelled, "What's wrong?"

His mom didn't answer. The rest of the silent ride home, his mom drove even slower than usual. When they finally arrived home, his mom grabbed him before he was halfway out of the car. With a strength Ahlwynn had no idea his mother possessed, she lifted him up as though he were still a little kid. Her arms squeezed him with the same superhuman strength.

"Mom, that hurts!"

She sat him down. "I'm sorry, it's just that, if anything, if," She straightened out his hair. "Sorry, I almost forgot."

She looked at the back door, an expression Ahlwynn couldn't fathom on her face, "Let's go in."

Grabbing his backpack from the backseat, Ahlwynn ran into the house. "Auntie, I'm having an overnighter!" Throwing his backpack onto the couch, he rushed to his room. "I'm calling Tim right now. We need to make plans!"

Leaving his door open, he punched Tim's number on the cell phone. It went straight to voice mail. A second later a text arrived. *'Can't talk'*

He heard his mom say, "Oh, Kaye, I'm so sorry—"

Kaye interrupted, "No, I'm the one who should be sorry, begging for your forgiveness!"

Elaine stared at her baby sister. *What does Kaye have to be sorry about? I attacked her, called her a tramp and worse.*

Kaye kept talking, "You have always given me good advice. I never listened. You're right! Oh, Elaine, if our parents knew what a slut I've become! If I'm to keep a good man like *Edward* around, it is time to clean up my act."

Elaine thought, *Little sister, I didn't care if you cleaned up your act; I wanted you out of my act.* Out loud Elaine said, "I was too harsh."

Kaye cut in. "No, you weren't. Your Dragon Lady speech was just what I needed. Just like when your inner Dragon Lady negotiated with Mr. Strange. You made him promise to pay more than a thousand. You said the right words, the right way. A pair of awesome women like us, doing the specialty work we do, at his beck and call; we are worth more. I am worth more. No more cheap and easy Kaye. I am going to be a high class Dragon Lady, just like you!"

THE MOPSTERS

Elaine looked at Kaye, standing with a pride not shown for years. *Little sister, if wanting Edward can change you so much...* Elaine felt herself melting, wanting to let Kaye have anything she desired. *I demanded better pay to keep Ahlwynn in Kathy's School. I inspired you get some self-respect. Will I ever unleash my Inner Dragon Lady to get me what I want?*

Elaine wanted Edward.

Kaye, just looking at you, it is obvious why men desire you. If you start growing up as superior emotionally as you have physically, Edward won't know what hit him. Jealousy twisted within Elaine, overwhelmed the guilt she felt from her almost-accident. *This time I will take...* Elaine censored her own ugly thoughts.

Deliberately changing the subject, Elaine said. "Kaye, let's see if you are still so grateful this Friday. I got a text from Mr. Strange to keep Friday, and maybe Saturday, clear, details coming later."

Kaye laughed. "Can't be any worse than the first one!"

Watching from his room, Ahlwynn was relieved to see his mom and aunt acting normal.

Soon dinner aroma filled the air.

The usual silly jokes filled dinner conversation.

Ahlwynn even enjoyed washing dishes after dinner.

When bedtime came, he tried to imagine what it would be like to sleep in a strange room. Just as he was about to doze off, he heard his Mom's phone ring.

He heard his mother. "Edward! We had a great time yesterday."

Her voice changed. "Yes, no problem. I understand... Two weeks? ...Then when?... Well, let me know... Uh, fine. No, really. ... Bye."

"Kaye, that was Edward. He will be out of town longer than expected, trouble with current client. He'll let us know when he can do dinner again."

Kaye asked, "Brush off?"

Ahlwynn couldn't understand what his mom said.

Kaye said, "Or perhaps back together with someone, like a wife? I knew he was too good to be true!"

Again, Ahlwynn couldn't understand what his mom said.

Kaye said, "Elaine, wake up and smell the pond scum!"

This time Ahlwynn could easily hear his mom shout at Kaye. "You have dated so many pond scum rejects; you don't understand a decent man can have an honest change of plans!"

Kaye said, "We will see."

Elaine said, "Right, we will. But no matter what Edward does, we have something more important. Sisters are forever. You and Ahlwynn are all I need."

Ahlwynn's last thought as he fell asleep, *Good, Mom will stay a mom.*

Hours later, Kaye's last thought before dozing, *I hope 'Laney's right. Edward's such a good dancer, and so cute.*

Elaine's last thought as she drifted into tormented slumber, *I must be an idiot to keep defending a man I hardly know.* She imagined Edward next to her.

Episode 9: Secrets to Share

Friday morning Ahlwynn woke and dressed an hour earlier than usual. His mom and aunt still asleep, Ahlwynn tiptoed to the kitchen, where his new sleeping bag leaned against the back door, ready to pick up when he left for school. He snatched the bag and rushed with it to his room, deliberating 'forgetting' his mother's final words the night before, "Stop playing with that, or you'll wear it out before you ever use it!"

Putting the sleeping bag on his bed, Ahlwynn unrolled it. He admired the way its dark blue reflected the light. He rubbed his hand over its sleek surface. He and his mom had spent hours searching for just the right bag. He feared he would never be able to pick out which style he liked best until his mother had shown him this model had secret pockets that would let him store everything in it, no need for a suitcase. Then it was down to deciding which color. This blue reminded Ahlwynn of star filled skies.

Grabbing the list he had written the night before, Ahlwynn reviewed it as meticulously as if he were an astronaut heading for a distant planet with no chance for a resupply.

Toothpaste, check

Toothbrush, check

Clean underwear, check

Brand new pajamas, never worn, check

Brand new Levis, check

Bran new t-shirt, with picture of Einstein sticking his tongue out, check

F. E. TABOR AND FRAN TABOR

Latest Avengers comic book, check
Cell phone charger, check
Cell phone, check

All of which were jammed into the 'secret pockets' of his very first sleeping bag ever.

He heard his mother's alarm clock ring. Double checking that everything was properly stowed away, he quickly rolled the bag and secured its straps. He rushed it to the back door. He had just put it down when his mother stepped out of her bedroom.

Elaine said, "I'm glad you aren't unrolling that again."

Ahlwynn, with his best 'innocent' face, said, "Of course not, Mom. Can we skip breakfast? You don't want to be late for work."

Kaye came out of her room. "Did I hear Ahlwynn ask to skip breakfast?"

Elaine laughed. "You did." She looked at her son. "No matter how early you get to school, you won't get to Tim's house one minute sooner. There's plenty of time for oatmeal." Wetting her hand from the kitchen sink, she patted down her son's hair. "That's better."

Ahlwynn protested, "Mom!"

Elaine was both relieved and disappointed Ahlwynn wanted to get to school early. From Ahlwynn's first newborn wail, he had not spent even one night away from her. Now he was spending the night with a family she didn't even know. *What was I thinking? I could have sent Kaye to pick him up. Ahlwynn could have helped.*

Monday, Elaine had not yet learned the exact address of this week's Mr. Strange cleaning job, only that it was about an hour drive from the school. *Leaving the job to get Ahlwynn and bring him back would take Kaye at least two hours. No way Ahlwynn's help could make up for the lost time. Or could it? When sweet grandmotherly types weren't stuffing him with cookies, my son was a big help. Did I make the wrong choice?*

Elaine remembered the trashed room full of deep holes poked into every wall, the result of a dangerous lawn dart fight. *I've seen what*

THE MOPSTERS

spoiled rich people can do! What if Tim has lawn-dart-throwing older brothers or cousins? Does Tim even have brothers or sisters? What kind of mother sends her child on an overnighter with total strangers?

Elaine, trying to sound casual, asked, "Does Tim have any brothers or sisters?"

Ahlwynn answered, "Naw, he's an only child like me."

Elaine felt relieved. *No older lawn-dart-throwing siblings.* Then she asked herself, *Why only one child? Do they hate children, Tim their one 'accident'? I don't even know if Tim's mom is married! I've had all week to ask these questions; instead I've been shopping so my son will look good for strangers! I am a bad mom!*

She asked, "What is Tim's father like?" *Please don't say Tim has an evil stepdad, or his mom lives with boyfriends.*

Ahlwynn, already slurping up his instant oatmeal, said, "His dad is really cool. One reason Tim knows so much about robots is his dad invents specialized robots he sells to big companies. Tim said his dad has a whole shop in their basement, filled with shelves stacked to the ceiling with electronics. Tim said his dad promised he would show me some cool top secret stuff after dinner dishes."

Kaye asked, "Dinner dishes?"

Ahlwynn said, "Tim complains his dad thinks one of things wrong with modern kids is they don't have enough chores, so he makes Tim help their cook with dishes every night. Think, all that money and Tim still has to do the same boring work I do."

Kaye asked, "Their cook?"

Ahlwynn said, "Ya, like you use to do for the Simpson's, only their cook cooks every night."

Kaye, her voice trailing off, whispered, "A cook..."

Elaine felt relief. *Doesn't sound like the families I clean up after. What could go wrong?*

Ahlwynn's overnighter started as planned.

Tim's mom picked them up on time. When they finally reached Tim's home, Ahlwynn stared. He knew Tim's house would be big, but Ahlwynn had no idea a driveway could be so long.

Dinner was a different kind of fun than dinner at home, no silly talking. Doing dishes with the cook wasn't much different than doing dishes with his Mom. The cook supervised as he and Tim did everything, even the pots and pans, by hand. Tim explained nights when there was lots of company, the cook used both dishwashers, one for the pots and pans and another for the regular dishes. Those nights, sometimes he helped, but usually not.

After finally finishing the dishes, they went to the basement where Tim's dad waited for them.

Walking around shelves housing electronic components, dial and gauge covered metal boxes, and lots of other paraphernalia found in typical mad scientist movies, Ahlwynn felt like he had left earth and walked into heaven.

After giving the boys a tour of all the specialized equipment, Tim's dad reached up to a high shelf and brought down two boxes full of cut pieces of metal, screws and assorted electrical components. Handing a box to each boy he said, "These boxes contain all you need to build a robotic picking arm. Want to make one?"

Both boys yelled, "Yes!"

Ahlwynn asked what the robotic arms were to be used for. Tim's dad said, "They are to be used for fun. You get to keep the one you build."

The boys immediately started lining up components on workbench space that 'happened' to be empty.

Ahlwynn loved Vinny's fun spirit; he admired Edward's cool self-assurance. Tim's dad was like the best of both of them, and more. Although Ahlwynn had always wanted a real live father, he had never felt envious of others. Suddenly, the hole in Ahlwynn's life labeled 'father' grew larger.

THE MOPSTERS

When Tim's dad admired how well Ahlwynn handled a screwdriver, Ahlwynn started to pretend Tim's father was his own father. Ahlwynn's logical mind overpowered his story-telling mind. Ahlwynn thought, *'Borrowing' someone else's father is almost like stealing; secret stealing, but stealing.*

Each kit included a small soldering iron and a bundle of fine solder. Ahlwynn had used Vinny's big bulky soldering iron, but had never worked with such delicate components.

Tim's dad, noticing Ahlwynn's hesitancy, showed him how to use the tool. Ahlwynn quickly caught on. As he said thanks for the help, Ahlwynn thought, *If my dad had lived, I bet my real daddy would have been even nicer.*

Ahlwynn finished tightening down the final tiny screw. *My real Dad and I could have...* Tears started. He quickly wiped them away with the back of his sleeve; he glanced at Tim.

Tim concentrated intently on his own project. He never looked up, never noticed.

By the time Tim finished, Ahlwynn's tears were gone.

When Ahlwynn claimed he had finished almost the exact same time Tim had, Tim believed him.

Tim's father noticed Ahlwynn's greater understanding, and his tears, but said, "You two are both grade A engineers! Let's go upstairs for some celebratory hot chocolate!"

Several cups of cocoa and an hour later, the two boys were told it was bedtime. Tim was elated he did not have to sleep in his bed but instead got to sleep on the floor in his indoor sleeping bag, just like Ahlwynn.

Tim's mother insisted they leave the door partially open so Ahlwynn could see where he was in case he woke up in the middle of the night.

As soon as the boys heard her walk away, they started whispering about school, the basement workshop, the Avengers and the possibility of real live extraterrestrials.

Thinking the boys were finally asleep, Tim's parents had a small glass of wine together. The parents agreed Ahlwynn seemed like a nice boy, but a bit 'tight'. He obviously had trouble relaxing. They both agreed there was something wrong with a boy who cried for no reason.

Giving his wife a quick peck on the cheek, Tim's dad went downstairs to work. Alice knew he would lose all track of time, work through the night and still be working while everybody else ate breakfast.

Heading for her room, she was surprised to hear conversation from Tim's room. She heard "...was a thousand a day, now when they do strange calls, it's more."

Alice froze, listened harder. She heard her son, her innocent son, mumble something about why when Ahlwynn's mom gets calls from strange men, she can't wait to collect although "it's dirty work."

She heard Ahlwynn explain not everyone is willing to get as dirty as his mom and Aunt Kaye, but they were the best and worth it. "They make lots of money doing it."

Alice fought the urge to burst in. *Tomorrow, after Ahlwynn leaves, Tim will have a father and son talk; explaining what makes some women not nice is a father's job. Poor Ahlwynn, he doesn't seem to understand his mother is pure trash. Now I know why someone with scrub-woman hands has the money to put her kid in Kathy's School. Monday morning, I tell Kathy the facts. Kathy will contact social services about poor Ahlwynn.*

Alice felt sorry for 'poor Ahlwynn', but she decided there would be no more overnighters, at least not with a child of a prostitute. Dare she tell her son Ahlwynn can't be his friend anymore? Tim had been so happy to have a friend his own age who understood robots and loved science stuff as much as he did. *Tim can still play with Ahlwynn*

THE MOPSTERS

at school, just not too often. If social services took Ahlwynn away, a real possibility, life would be so much simpler.

Alice went to bed, satisfied she had made all the right decisions. After all, she was nothing if not fair.

Episode 10: Secrets Shared

The next morning Alice could hardly wait for that weird boy to be gone, out of her house.

Noon came. No one came.

One o'clock. No one. One-thirty, Two o'clock.

Alice wasn't really surprised. *Just like trash to have no sense of time.*

Finally that ratty station wagon with the tacky "The Mopsters" logo plastered on its sides appeared. It crept up the long drive. Alice waited for it to arrive at the house. She rushed out to greet Elaine.

Elaine plodded up the front walk.

Alice noted how Elaine's normally neat hair had random strands sticking out at odd angles. Her sweat stained blouse was only partially tucked in; its top button, missing. Thread still dangled from where the button should have been. Obviously, the button had been torn off. *Probably in a moment of illicit passion.* Equally obvious, Elaine had thrown her clothes on in a hurry, after sleeping in from her night's 'work.'

Elaine said, "Sorry I'm so late. Yesterday's job was easily the worst I've had! Kaye and I slept over so we could get at it again first thing this morning."

For the first time Alice noticed another woman still in the car, her thick hair plastered against the rolled up window. Pointing, Alice asked, "That Kaye?"

Elaine said, "Yes. She's passed out. Working all night is exhausting."

Tim and Ahlwynn came to the door. Ahlwynn said, "Mom, see the cool robot arm I made! Can I spend another night? Tim has some rad ideas for how we can make our robot arms work together!"

Before anyone else could say anything, Alice said, "That's impossible. Get your stuff together right away so your mother can take you home. It looks like she needs some sleep. Real sleep."

Elaine said, "Too true." She turned to her son. "Let's get your sleeping bag." She started to follow her son.

Alice stood like a sentinel, blocking Elaine's way. "He will be right back. You should relax. Wait in the car."

Disappointed she wouldn't get to see the inside of the elegant home, but relieved she could sit, get some weight off her feet, Elaine said, "OK." She shuffled back to her car.

ALL THE WAY HOME AHLWYNN talked excitedly about all the things he and Tim did. He couldn't wait to show cousin Vinny the robot arm he had made.

Elaine felt relief. *What was I worried about?* Glancing at her son's happy face in the rear view mirror, she smiled to herself. *He has a best friend; they have overnighters, share comic books and build things. I don't care how many disaster houses I have to clean up, it's worth it to finally be able to give my son a real childhood.*

MONDAY MORNING ALICE dropped Tim off for school, but didn't drive off. She parked the car and followed her son in.

Tim rushed to his classroom, hoping his mom wouldn't follow.

She didn't; she headed for Kathy's office.

Good. He had no intention of following her advice, to quit spending so much time with his best friend.

THE MOPSTERS

Tim thought of the confusing talk he had with his father. His dad stuttered. Tim had never heard him stutter before. His dad stuttered and mumbled something about good girls and nice girls and a repeated "You will understand someday." His dad had acted so relieved when Tim said, "Dad, I already know not everyone is nice. You said you would show me your latest project." His dad quit stuttering; the rest of the afternoon was fun.

Parents could be so strange.

ALICE MARCHED INTO Kathy's office and closed the door behind her. "Kathy, you are not just the principal of my son's school, you are one of my oldest and dearest friends."

Kathy looked up from the stack of bills on her desk. She tried to smile. "Hi, Alice."

Alice sat down on the chair in front of Kathy's desk, pulled it closer. Alice leaned forward. "I bet you have wondered how such commoners as Elaine and her sister can afford your school. Even with a partial scholarship, it should be out of their reach."

Kathy started to say something, but stopped. She waited for Alice to speak.

Alice shared all she had learned, including the disheveled mess Elaine was when she finally picked up her son, hours late.

Kathy thanked her for the information; it explained some of the odd behaviors Ahlwynn exhibited.

As soon as Alice left, Kathy called her brother. "Edward, you know that lady you are seeing? Well I just learned something you should know about her and her sister. They might clean a few houses, but that is just a cover for their real occupation, the world's oldest profession."

Edward protested she must be wrong.

Kathy said, "Edward, you might be a 'wise guy' when you are on the job, but in your private life you keep falling for super sluts wearing fake angel wings."

Edward said, "Be careful. You could be talking about your future sister-in-law."

Kathy said, "Was I wrong about your last girl friend?"

Edward protested, "No, but this time you are. I can't talk more, this case is getting hot. I won't be taking calls all week, maybe two. Don't do anything rash. Trust me."

Kathy hung up. *Just like last time. Will my baby brother ever learn?*

EDWARD STARED AT THE silent, black screen on his phone. He thought of Kaye's forward ways, what she had done with her bare feet during the first dinner he had with her family. Had Ahlwynn's normalcy, the obvious need for a real father type in his life, the tragedy of his mother widowed on what should have been a day of rejoicing, had all that blinded him? Could Kathy be right?

He took a deep breath. Thinking about women had distracted more than a few of his colleagues, distracted them into an early grave. His sister, right or wrong; his new hope of love, true or false; he had work to do.

In two weeks, if he were still alive, he would learn the truth. Until then...He sent a text to Kaye's phone. "Tight negotiations. Will call when in town, 2 weeks. Until then, no communication."

He set his phone to not respond to Elaine or Kaye's number. Any call attempts or texts would now go straight to his home computer, to be looked at only when his current assignment was completed.

ELAINE AND KAYE PICKED up Ahlwynn on schedule.

THE MOPSTERS

As Ahlwynn slipped into the backseat, his Mom asked him, "How was your day?"

"Fine."

Kaye said, "Glad it was fine for someone."

Elaine snapped at her sister, "That's enough. Stop beating a dead horse!"

Ahlwynn, staring out the window, asked, "Dead horse?"

Kaye answered, "Edward sent a text, saying he can't talk to us or anything for two weeks, and when I tried to call him back, it went straight to voice mail. I knew he was too good to be true."

Elaine shouted at her sister, "You've been repeating that all day. If he's such a lost cause, call up one of your old boyfriends!"

Kaye said, "Save your shouting for Edward. He is the one hiding something."

Elaine said, "He told us he did hush-hush work for demanding big corporations."

Kaye said, "A perfect cover for a travels-a-lot married man."

Elaine said, "He doesn't seem married."

Kaye sighed, "His kind never do, especially the really good looking ones."

Ahlwynn repeated, "What about the horse?"

Elaine, using the rear view mirror to look at her son, asked, "Horse?"

"You told Auntie to stop beating a dead horse."

The sisters laughed. His mom explained, "That's an old expression, it means to stop complaining about the same thing over and over, just rehashing old arguments that never go anywhere."

"Oh." He resumed staring out the window.

Elaine nodded at her sister, pointed with her chin towards Ahlwynn. It took Kaye a moment to catch on, but when she looked back at Ahlwynn she understood.

Ahlwynn sat slouched over, staring outside with the same listless expression he so often had when leaving his old school.

Kaye frowned, glanced at her sister. She mouthed, "Why?"

Elaine shrugged. "Ahlwynn, anything unusual happen at school today."

"No." Silence. "Mom?"

"Yes?"

"Today Tim told me he was going to stay my friend, no matter what his mom said. Like it was some big deal. When I asked him why, he said he didn't care what you did." He looked up at the rear view mirror; it framed his mom's eyes. "Mom, I don't care what anybody says, if they don't like you or what you do, I don't like them."

Kaye and Elaine exchanged a quick look. Kaye muttered under her breath, "Snobs!"

Elaine asked, "Did you tell Tim that?"

"No, it took a while to figure out what he meant, or why I felt yucky inside when he said it. It felt yuckier than when mean old Ms. Charley called me a freak." He kicked the back of the seat. "I knew old Charley didn't like me."

Kaye asked, "What else did Tim say?"

Ahlwynn kicked again. "Just that his mom told him to stay polite, but stop being good friends. Something about trash women have trash kids, but he didn't believe it." Ahlwynn kicked the back of the car seat again. "I should have hit him."

Elaine's eyes got big. "You are not to hit anyone!" *Next time I see that snob Alice I just might ignore my own advice. Maybe a big black eye would force her to see reason! I clean up trash, but trash people don't work like I work.* Thinking about slugging Alice, picturing that pompous, overdressed, underhanded, backbiting snooty bitch landing in a giant, slimy mud puddle, felt embarrassingly good. *My son was finally happy. That self-righteous bitch will not get away with hurting him!*

Elaine asked, "What did you say to Tim?"

THE MOPSTERS

"Not much. He said he'd call me tonight about his dad's latest secret robot, but I'm not to call him."

Kaye said, "Another don't-call-me scenario. Today, hiding calls from his mom; tomorrow he will be hiding calls from his wife."

Elaine said, "Kaye, that's enough!" Elaine remembered how excitedly Ahlwynn talked about Tim's dad. "Did Tim say his dad told him to stop being friends?"

Ahlwynn said, "No, Tim said his dad didn't make much sense at all. He rambled on about how women like you are more necessary to a smooth running society than most people acknowledge."

Elaine said, "Well, at least his father isn't a money-proud snob like his mother. Ahlwynn, good friends tell the truth, even when they are afraid of what you might think. Tim is a good friend. His mother is not a nice person, but she is Tim's mom and an adult. Do you know what that means?"

"Yes, Mom. I have to treat her with respect." He paused. "Then it's OK if Tim and I remain friends?"

Elaine flipped her hair, gave her shoulders a haughty wiggle and, with her nose in the air, her voice deep and her accent British, said, "Tim's mom is such a low class person. Not a surprise she does not comprehend we cleaning ladies are essential to a smooth running society. Do not let her obvious inferiority cloud your friendship with Tim. Do let him remain your best friend."

Ahlwynn and Kaye both giggled.

For the first time, Ahlwynn noticed a plastic bag in the back part of the wagon. A dry cleaner's label hung from it. As he reached for it he asked, "What's this?"

"What does it look like?"

Ahlwynn pulled it out of its clear plastic wrapper. "A hat."

It was a pale purple with a shiny band. The label inside said 100% wool.

Elaine laughed. "I knew you were smart, now you just proved it. It's a fedora, like was popular about a hundred years ago. Back then, a proper man would no more leave the house without his hat than he would without his pants. Though I doubt many men wore that color back then."

Ahlwynn tried it on. It was a bit large, but he didn't mind. "Whose is it?"

Elaine started to answer, but Kaye interrupted her. "Yours. The last house we did, that all-nighter, we were told they were selling the place, to toss any clothing items. That hat was just outside the house, caked with dried on mud, so we dropped it off at the dry cleaners. I thought you would like it. Do you?"

"Do I? It is cool!"

Unnoticed by Ahlwynn, his mom mouthed to Kaye, "Thanks." Kaye mouthed back, "No problem."

Ahlwynn pulled the hat to an angle, "OK, you thugs, I'm taking you in."

Kaye laughed. "No FBI agent could have said it better."

Ahlwynn asked, "Can I wear it to school?"

Kaye said, "You can wear it wherever, whenever you want." She reached into the glove box, pulled out the tip of a peacock feather. "This was in the band when we found it. The only part not dirty."

Ahlwynn stuck the feather tip into the band. The dark peacock 'eye' contrasted with the felt fedora's purple. He held the hat at different angles, admired the feather's changing iridescence. "Now it is even cooler."

Episode 11: High Fashion

The next day Ahlwynn wore his new hat to school. At recess everyone wanted to try it on; arguments started over who was next.

Ahlwynn discovered having something no one else had, and everyone wanted, felt good. Real good.

That afternoon a reporter doing a human interest story on local school playgrounds spotted Ahlwynn in his hat. After first verifying Ahlwynn's guardians had given permission for his picture to be used in school publicity shots, the reporter took several pictures of Ahlwynn climbing over and through the school's large metal climbing sculpture. Ahlwynn found the reporter's repeated "Smile big!" reminders annoying.

Ahlwynn heard the reporter say the purple hat added "color and an interesting difference" to his pictures and video. From the top of the climbing sculpture Ahlwynn spotted Tim.

Tim envied him!

The reporter no longer had to remind Ahlwynn to "Smile big."

That evening, Ahlwynn, his mom and his aunt sat together watching the local "What's Happening in Our Town" episode about modern changes in school playgrounds. When it finally got to the three seconds showing Ahlwynn on top of Kathy's School climbing sculpture, all three yelled and cheered. At the end of the episode, the anchor said, "For additional information and pictures, go to our station's website."

Ahlwynn raced to his room to retrieve his school laptop. With his Mom and Auntie looking over his shoulders, he quickly opened the right website and strolled through the offerings, found one labeled 'playgrounds.'

Opening it, they discovered hundreds of playground pictures from all over town. There were at least a dozen more pictures of Ahlwynn than any other child.

Kaye said, "Ahlwynn, you are one good looking nephew. You clearly got your good looks from me."

Elaine mock-protested, "Ahem! Mother speaking here. You had nothing to do with it. I am clearly the one who gave him his good looks."

Ahlwynn laughed. "Stop fighting. Mom, you gave me my good looks. Kaye, you gave me the hat." He stood. Using the hat to accentuate his broad, sweeping gesture, he bowed to the two sisters. "Madams, I salute you both. Without the hat, I would have been just one more incredibly handsome young man in the crowd; just one pretty face among many."

He bowed to his mother. "Thank you, Mom, for the genetics."

He turned to his aunt, held the hat over his heart. "And thank you Auntie, for the hat. Mom mentioned while fixing dinner you planned to keep it for yourself. We can take turns wearing it. Deal?"

Kaye said, "Deal. Tomorrow, my turn."

Ahlwynn thought, *So soon?* His voice lower, "Sure, tomorrow's fine."

Kaye laughed. "Tomorrow we will be cleaning Mrs. Green's place, not a dress up time."

The next day at school, everyone wanted a turn to wear Ahlwynn's hat, but they no longer lined up for the privilege.

THE MOPSTERS

WHEN THE SISTERS ARRIVED at Mrs. Green's house, she met them at the door with a big smile. "I saw young master Ahlwynn on TV last night! He looked so dashing!"

As Elaine thanked her for the compliment, her phone rang. A text from Kathy. 'Please stop by my office today. Before school lets out. Text back if can.'

Mrs. Green said, "I bet she wants to rave about your movie star son."

Elaine said, "Or share his latest antics." She texted back, '2:30 work?'

'Perfect'

Elaine said, "If we are to get done in time, we better start working."

Mrs. Green said, "Before you leave, be sure to take the book on the kitchen table. It is another of my brother's old books I think Ahlwynn will like. Now I'm off on my doctor mandated constitutional." She left.

Elaine and Kaye started cleaning. The elderly lady's house, as usual, was so clean they had no trouble finishing early.

Elaine pulled up to the school just after two. "Let's go see what Kathy wants us for."

Kaye said, "I never did like going to the principal's office, you go see. Me, I'll just check out the scenery."

Elaine took her time walking into the school. She admired student artwork in the hallway. She discreetly peaked through the windowed doors, watching classrooms in action. Two-thirty on the dot, she knocked on Kathy's door. "You wanted to see me?"

Kathy looked up from her paperwork. "Yes. Normally I would be in a classroom this time of day, but I left my assistant in charge so we can talk alone."

Elaine said, "Is there a problem with the scholarship? Did my son say or do something bad?"

Kathy said, "Ahlwynn's a charmer. Sit down. We need to talk."

Elaine pulled a wooden chair closer to the desk's front. "Talk?"

Kathy said, "Ahlwynn is charming." She looked away from Elaine.

Elaine said, "But."

Kathy questioned, "But?"

Elaine said, "You are about to tell me my son is charming, *but* there is a problem. Look, I don't care how active or too talkative he is, no one is putting my son on drugs!"

Kathy's eyes went wide. "Drugs? Of course not! Ahlwynn is the type of child this school is made for. He's fine. It's you."

Elaine said, "Me?"

Kathy nodded.

Elaine leaned forward, "I can give you part of the sign up fee right now. If you just wait like you promised, I will have the rest. You have my word. Whatever it takes. My son loves this school."

Kathy said, "It's not the money. It's how you earn your money." Kathy looked down at her desk. "You must realize, your profession, it is not the norm."

Elaine snapped, "Not the norm? Has Alice, Tim's mom, been talking to you?"

Kathy's voice dropped, "You must understand. Alice has standards, expectations. She doesn't object to what you do, she just doesn't think socializing—"

Elaine interrupted. "To use her husband's own words, woman in my profession are much more important to a smooth running society than most people think!"

Kathy's eyes went wide. "*He* said that?"

Elaine said, "Yes, and he is right. You would not believe the filth that would build up if not for the services I offer."

Kathy mumbled, "Build up?"

Elaine continued, "Even the most dedicated housewife needs a break. Some men are so demanding, their wives call me just to get some relief."

Kathy spluttered, "I didn't know."

THE MOPSTERS

Elaine, her 'inner dragon lady' fully aroused, replied, "You are right. You don't know. Kaye and I work hard. Sometimes, when we get extreme clients, we do things no one should have to do. But we do it. Know why?"

Kathy shook her head no.

"Because it has to be done. By someone. I value my son's education more than I hate getting a little dirty."

Elaine stood, her hands on the desk, leaning over Kathy, who instinctively leaned back. Elaine, her voice lower, "My son is staying in this school. You will not let some sanctimonious, self-righteous snob push him out. Do we understand each other?"

Kathy nodded.

"Good." Elaine sat down, smiled, "Anything else?"

Kathy took a deep breath. "Yes, there is one other thing. Nothing to do with your son, or the school. It's my brother. I understand he's been to your house a couple times."

Elaine said, "So?"

Kathy said, "This is nothing about you. My brother is a big boy, he can see whom he wants, but sometimes people get hurt."

Elaine questioned, "Get hurt?"

Kathy said, "Edward isn't always wise when it comes to women. He will date several at a time. He's a good man, mostly. Look, I know woman in your profession can get fantasies about a successful man marrying them, changing their lives. He has given others that idea."

Elaine's eyes narrowed. "You don't think I'm good enough for him, so you are warning me off?"

Kathy paused, forced herself to take a deep breath before replying, "I am not 'warning you off.' I am being prudent. If you and your sister had a falling out with my brother, your anger could extend to me. From me, to this school. My school."

Elaine said, "Like you said, your brother is a big boy. I am an adult woman. I don't think either of us needs personal advice. Anything else?"

Kathy said, "No."

Elaine stood, turned towards the door.

Kathy said, "Elaine?"

Elaine turned back.

"Please understand. I have nothing personal against your profession. I respect all working women."

Elaine said, "But you respect some more than others." Slamming the door behind her, she left.

Alone in her office, Kathy said, "Shouldn't I?"

ELAINE MARCHED INTO the hallway, oblivious to all but her swirling thoughts. Alice's snobbery angered her. At the same time she felt guardedly elated. *Kathy wouldn't try to warn me off Edward unless he liked me; unless I have a chance...* She marched right into a strange man. He fell.

Elaine, "I'm sorry!" She helped him up.

The man brushed himself off. "You must be Elaine. I was just talking to your sister. I'm Timothy senior, Tim's dad."

Elaine stared at him.

"I'm here to make sure Alice, my wife, didn't cause any trouble."

Elaine said, "I think she asked Kathy to have my son kicked out of school because of how I earn a living."

"You have to forgive Alice. She tries so hard to fit into her idea of high society. I tried to tell her people aren't as judgmental about that sort of thing as they use to be."

Elaine said, "As long as she doesn't spread her ideas around, or make my son uncomfortable or ashamed of his family, I will be a lot more tolerant than she is."

THE MOPSTERS

Timothy senior started to stutter, "G-g-good. S-s-sometime. G-g-guess not. Need to see Kathy, let her know I want Ahlwynn to stay. My son needs a friend like him." He went into Kathy's office without knocking.

Elaine found her sister meandering around the latest art displays.

Kaye said, "I just had the strangest conversation with Tim's dad. He kept saying how people undervalue the importance of women like me. Then he started to ask something about how I work; then he got all red. I think I know why he has only one child. He has to be the shyest man alive!"

Elaine said, "According to Kathy, someone else isn't so shy. She claims Edward is a womanizing two-timer."

Kaye said, "I knew it!"

Elaine said, "Or was she lying because she doesn't want her brother socializing with common scrub women like us?"

Kaye said, "She's known what we do for a living since we turned in those scholarship applications. She's not an Alice type snob."

Elaine described the conversation she had.

Kaye said, "If anyone makes trouble for my nephew!"

A rush of children interrupted them; school was out.

A cheerful Ahlwynn came out of his classroom. When he spotted his mom, his expression saddened. "You're early! Now Tim and I don't have time to play!"

Elaine thought, *It's worth the work, the putting up with the Alice's of the world, to see you so happy you don't want to leave.* She remembered too well the trapped animal look her son had almost every day at his old school. She said, "You wouldn't have had time anyway. Tim's dad is here, too."

Episode 12: True Trash

Early the next morning Kathy called Elaine. Someone had vandalized the school and broken into her office. Did they have anything to do with it? It took several minutes, but Elaine finally convinced her she had nothing to do with it.

When they drove up to the school, a police car sat in front of the school. Broken glass lay scattered across the front of the school. Student artwork was strewn across the hallway floor. Kathy's office, records thrown everywhere, was trashed.

Kathy mentioned when she first came to work, discovered the disaster; the building had a "sour" smell. She was relieved a few open windows handled the smell, but she had no idea where to start cleaning. Fortunately the classrooms were not touched, and each could be safely accessed from the back playground.

Elaine said, "We have a day off today. Sis and I will clean up this mess."

Kathy stared at her. "Oh, I guess you do that too."

Elaine replied, "You're in shock. Don't worry. Kaye and I have seen worse."

Elaine asked the police when it would be OK to start cleaning up the mess. She was shocked when the officer said now was fine. She asked, "Don't you need to look for clues or something?"

"No, not for ordinary vandalism. People get jealous, they take it out on someone or something they think has it better than they do. We see it all the time. This is nothing."

Elaine went back to her car. "Grab our totes, Kaye. We are cleaning here today."

Kaye said, "Today was supposed to be our day off." She grabbed a tote and followed her sister into the school. She looked around and shook her head. "A Mr. Strange level of cleaning, and no Mr. Strange money." She looked at her sister. "Or is there?"

Elaine, walking back to the car for the next load, said, "We are doing this free gratis. Proving the world needs us cleaning types."

Kaye's eyebrows arched. "The world? Or one snotty somebody?" She grabbed the final tote.

Elaine, pulling the big broom out of their Subaru, said, "Maybe several snotty somebodies."

By the time Elaine and Kaye finished removing the last public signs of the vandalism, the school day was also finishing.

Kathy's private office proved to be a special challenge. Not only was the desk upended and a chair broken, but the vandals took a special delight shredding, tossing and crumbling nearly every piece of paper in every file cabinet. Elaine piled color-sorted shredded pages into several boxes. She remembered a movie in which small children helped identify secret agents by assembling strips of paper. In the movie, what should have been a fun children's puzzle, became a life and death challenge.

The many scrambled strips of paper Elaine salvaged were not life and death; it would be up to Kathy if they were important enough to attempt reassembly.

The papers not run through the office shredder, even the torn ones, were easy to sort by type. Elaine had several stacks. She alphabetized the shortest pile and was about to start alphabetizing another one when Kathy walked in.

Kathy said, "I don't know what I would have done without your help. School had to go on. Emergency professional cleaners are not in

THE MOPSTERS

the budget. You and your sister are lifesavers. Thank you, and forgive my earlier self-righteous judgmentalism."

Elaine said, "You're forgiven. But whoever did this," She looked around the now immaculate but severely paper-cluttered office as though she could still see the hateful destruction. "That piece of trash is not forgiven. And I don't buy the cop's 'some jealous poor kid' line either. I've seen the damage spoiled rich kids do. My money says some overindulged, under-disciplined brat with no respect for property, his own or other's, did this."

Kathy blinked. "In your line of work, I bet you meet a lot of people who think money can bury any mistake they make."

Elaine shook her head. "You don't know the half of it. But I don't talk about my clients' secret lives."

Kathy nodded, blinked again as she stared at the woman before her. *From her application I learned Elaine is ten years younger than I am. Before I read her application I assumed she was older. I bet she was once beautiful. She's intelligent, hardworking. What leads a woman like her to prostitution? Being a real part time cleaning lady on the side is brilliant cover, but like Edward tells me, no cover lasts forever. What will happen to her son when her cover is unraveled?*

Kathy said, "No professional woman betrays a client's secrets. Not a teacher, not a..." Kathy paused. "Not a lady like you."

Elaine said, "Thank you." She resumed sorting the stack in front of her.

Kathy said, "I will finish that. Go home, relax a while."

"Thanks."

Kathy walked Elaine out. She felt a struggling-working-woman kinship with Elaine she had not felt with any of the other parents in her school. "I can't thank you enough. A small school like mine is more a labor of love than a business. Every month I fear I won't be able to make a critical payment. Every time it seems I'm about to get ahead, there is another improvement the building needs, or new supplies to buy or a staff member deserves and needs a raise. At this time, if I had had to pay for the work you and Kaye did today...the money wasn't there. It just is not there."

When they reached the car, Kathy went up to Kaye, shook her hand, and said, "Thank you."

Kathy looked down at Ahlwynn for several seconds before saying, "Your mother is a real lady, a good person. Don't ever stop believing that for any reason, no matter what anyone else says. Got it?"

Ahlwynn looked up at her. *Why do grownups prattle so much about the obvious?* "Got it."

As the rusty Subaru pulled away, Kathy turned to go back inside and to the massive paper sorting ahead of her.

Beep!

Annoyed, Kathy looked to see who was honking.

A shiny Toyota Land Rover pulled into the parking lot, Charlene! Kathy smiled. One of the friendliest and most generous of the parents, Charlene never failed to brighten her day. *After a day like today, I need some friendly conversation!*

Charlene got out of her Toyota. "Hi! Glad I caught you still here."

Kathy said, "I will be here a few more hours. What brings you by?"

Charlene said, "You, this school. My twins love it here."

Kathy said, "We love your little girls."

Charlene's twins were barely old enough for Kathy's school when they started last year, but admitting them had been as good a social decision as it was business. Charlene not only paid her tuition on time, but she singlehandedly contributed over ninety percent of their scholarship fund. Plus her friendly demeanor naturally made the school's few social events more fun. As if that weren't enough, Charlene's prestigious real estate investment firm attracted all the right people, resulting in a doubling of upper grade enrollments.

Charlene said, "I need to talk to you, alone."

THE MOPSTERS

Kathy said, "Come to my office. Do you mind if I do some brainless filing while we talk?"

Following Kathy into the building Charlene said, "If the filing is brainless enough, I can help you while we talk."

Kathy said, "Thank you, but this is something I better do myself. The papers include a lot of personal information."

When they entered Kathy's office, Charlene's eyes opened wide as she surveyed the boxes of torn official forms, stacks of papers, color-sorted paper strips from the shredding machine. "What happened?"

Kathy said, "You hadn't heard? We were vandalized last night. The vandals did a special number on my office. I'll be spending the night trying to get all our official paper records in order." She removed a box from the only extra chair, put it on the floor. "Sit."

Shocked, Charlene said, "This school?" She did a quick double take on the type of papers shredded. She remained standing.

Kathy said, "You didn't notice the police car when you dropped off your girls?"

Charlene said, "The nanny brought them today. Vandalisms just don't happen in this neighborhood."

Kathy said, "Hard to believe, but the officer said it happens everywhere, we just don't hear about it. What brings you by?" Kathy picked up the alphabetized stack. She began filing.

Charlene said, "I noticed the glass was missing from the hallway display case."

Kathy said, "There was broken glass everywhere. I don't know what I would have done without Elaine and Kaye's professional help?"

Charlene said, "Elaine and Kaye? The hookers?"

Kathy said, "They are professional housecleaners who work hard."

Charlene said, "Even with *my* donations, there is no way housecleaners can afford your school. Alice told me how they supplement their income."

137

Kathy said, "They are good people. I wouldn't have gotten through the day without their generous help."

Charlene said, "I have heard they are *very good* at what they do. Most of what they do involves being *friendly*. Kathy, in my line of work I meet people who make their living in many different, sometimes questionable, ways. I don't ask questions, but I do keep my eyes open. Kathy, I hate to say this, but women in their line of work attract bad people. Maybe, just maybe, your school got vandalized because one of their *associates* learned Ahlwynn attends this school."

Kathy said, "Why would that make a difference?"

Charlene sighed. "You don't understand criminals. Kathy, if Elaine suspected a connection between her son's attendance here and what happened to your school, what would she do? Did a guilty conscience motivate Elaine's generosity?"

Charlene clutched a pile of paper shreds. "Ordinary vandals toss papers, break glass, make a mess. Do common vandals bother to pull confidential files and run them through a paper shredder?" She waved the pom-pom like mass. "This is not ordinary vandalism. Kathy, Ahlwynn attending this school has brought it to the attention of a criminal element. I have to put the safety of my daughters ahead of all other considerations."

Charlene dropped her 'pom-poms,' grabbed the filing from Kathy's hand. She sat it firmly on the desk. She pushed the file shut. "Listen. Either those two women and their son never come back here, or I withdraw my daughters from this school. When they leave, my friends will pull their children out."

Kathy said, "Your friends first came here because of you, but they have all told me this school is the best thing that ever happened to their children. Your threats won't make me expel a wonderful student."

Charlene challenged, "Will the other parents keep their children in your school when I tell them why the vandals picked this school? You never had so much as graffiti before Ahlwynn showed up. Now, his

THE MOPSTERS

mother's enemies have attacked this school. If he stays, could they come during school hours?"

Kathy started to say something, but Charlene interrupted, this time her tonality pleading. "There might not be a connection. The vandalism might be a coincidence. Kathy, my little girls are only five. They would be so helpless if someone attacked this school. Other parents will be just as scared. Alice told me Ahlwynn is a nice boy; a bit strange, but nice. Children should not be punished for the sin of the parent; I don't like asking you to expel a nice boy. Kathy darling, my babies come first. Every parent will feel the same. If you want to keep your wonderful school going, you have no choice."

Kathy said, "Is that the only reason you stopped by tonight, to tell me you do not approve of Ahlwynn attending this school?"

Charlene said, "Alice and I talked about it. Ahlwynn's leaving would be for the best. My daughters love it here. I hate the idea of shopping for another school, but I will if you do not expel that boy." She stared hard at Kathy, her voice quietly firm. "What those hoodlums did can be fixed. Damage from my leaving, cannot be fixed."

Kathy felt energy drain from her. She collapsed onto the chair she had cleared for Charlene. She squeaked. "I know."

Charlene said, "Today is Ahlwynn's last day here?"

Kathy nodded yes.

"Good. See you tomorrow about the bake sale." Charlene left.

Kathy stared at her desk. *This room looked so bad. I don't know how Elaine and her sister were able to get so much done, so fast, but they are cleaning miracle workers. More important, I saw a side of Elaine...I was ready to tell my brother he is right about her. I like her. I like her sister. When I tell them Ahlwynn will not be allowed back, they will hate me almost as much as I hate myself. How was I ever fooled into thinking Charlene is a nice person?*

Suddenly Kathy sat up. "Wait a minute!" *Charlene wanted Ahlwynn gone before she knew about the school trashing! More important,*

Charlene has no trouble socializing with the 'wrong' people. Her wanting Ahlwynn out has nothing to do with his mom's side business or the fear of psychopaths attacking the children. Something else is going on. What?

She sent Edward a text. 'You solve mystery problems. Think I have one at school. Call or stop by as soon as you have time.'

Kathy got up, walked down the hallway. She studied the spotless display case that the day before had sliding glass doors. She remembered her horror-filled depression when she first saw the many glass shards covering the memorabilia within the case and spread over the floor. *If you didn't know yesterday the case had glass doors, you would never have guessed. In fact, it looks great just the way it now is. The floors look better than before the attack. Those sisters didn't work out of guilt; they were motivated by love.*

Back at her office, she resumed filing. She was surprised to discover she was humming. *Why am I so happy at practically guaranteeing my school will be bankrupted before the school year ends?*

But Kathy was happy, very happy, she did not call Elaine.

Ahlwynn was staying.

.

Episode 13: High Class Restaurant Trash?

On their way home, Kaye said, "Turn north on the highway."

Elaine asked, "Why?"

Kaye said, "I decided if we are rich enough to do a thousand dollar cleaning job for free, we are rich enough to treat ourselves. While you were talking to Kathy, I called Vinny, ordered a to-go, large, family sized lasagna, with all the trimmings, from that fancy restaurant he works at. It will soon be ready for pick up. I know dinner's an hour away, but we can stash it in the oven as soon as we get home and feast when we are ready."

Ahlwynn yelled, "Lasagna!"

Simultaneously, Elaine yelled, "*Antonio's* lasagna? Gold's cheaper!"

Kaye grinned, "Two out of three want lasagna. You will eat with us and you will like it."

Elaine sighed, "This once. Next time you plan a budget buster dinner, we talk first. OK?" Elaine looked over at her sister. "I presume I'm doing the buying?"

Kaye did her little-sister-mischief-maker grin. "This time I did the brain work, you get to do the leg work."

In the back seat, Ahlwynn laughed. "Just like you always say, Mom. Splitting the labor."

Elaine tried to look stern, but failed.

A short while later Elaine was in Antonio's sculpture and plant lined foyer, waiting for Vinny to bring her order. Peaking through layers of leaves, she admired the ornate interior and the well-dressed diners. She inhaled the spice-filled air, imagining she were at one of those tables, dating one of the handsome men, like the dark-suited mysterious one in the corner, with the splashy redhead. She watched the mystery man turn as he spoke to the waiter.

Edward!

Your sister tried to warn me, but I thought she was just trying to get me to back off.

Edward, not you! This side of town is not exactly out of town. So this is where you eat when not slumming with us!

That woman he was with was clearly one hundred percent tramp. Judging from the plate of food in front of him, Edward had a potbelly in his future. *How could anyone be interested in a slut-loving man doomed to go downhill?*

Jealous anger, betrayal, indignation, and other emotions she thought herself above, swirled from deep within the pit of Elaine's gut, tightened about her torso, and clamped even tighter around her throat. She gripped the plant, imagined throwing it across the room, trailing dirt on all the snow white table clothes, smashing into Edward's table, spraying tomato sauce and dirt over Edward and his date.

Elaine gripped the branches tighter, started to pull on the thick stem.

"Here, 'Laney."

Elaine released her grip, jumped back a step. "I didn't do anything!"

Cousin Vinny laughed at her. "Spyin' on the highfalutin clientele?"

Elaine said, "Uh, ya, curious, you know."

Vinny, spotlessly groomed, clean-shaven and dressed in Antonio's tuxedo-like wait staff uniform, carried two tall white paper bags full of Styrofoam encased yumminess. "This will taste just as good at home; maybe better."

THE MOPSTERS

Vinny thrust the full sacks into her arms. "When I first came to work here, those people intimidated me. Now, they're just people wanting to relax, have a good time, just like you and me."

Elaine wanted to ask about Edward. Did he come here often? Did he seem too friendly with his date? Instead she said, "Vinny, someday we are going to eat here, and maybe one of those people," She pointed with her chin towards the dining area. "Will be waiting on us." She pictured Edward, crawling on the floor, carrying a full tray of food, no not carrying food. Too dignified. On his hands and knees, as she used him like a bench while she ate her sloppy dinner, dribbling on him. Elaine smiled.

Vinny smiled back at her. "That would be fun, but I would rather take the food home, someplace I could relax. Gotta go!" He dashed back to the kitchen.

As Elaine walked back to her car, she wondered, *Should I tell Kaye tonight? Before or after dinner? Better not say anything in front of Ahlwynn. He's accustomed to men weaving in and out of Kaye's life. Edward will be just one more. If Ahlwynn knows Edward is a lying, two-timing, toad-faced scumbag, pond scum reject, he might say something should Edward show up at his sister's school. I'll ask Kaye to join me on a 'weight watcher's constitutional walk.' We'll need it after this meal. Ahlwynn does the dishes, so he can't join us.*

The heavy aroma of herb-rich lasagna enveloped her head, but Elaine's thoughts were so concentrated on Edward, she never noticed.

A couple hours later, all three of them leaned back from the table.

Kaye said, "I can't believe we ate the whole thing."

Ahlwynn said, "That was so-o-o-o-o good."

Elaine said, "Kaye, after all we have done lately, you are right. We deserved a break."

Ahlwynn said, "Those rolls were almost as good as the lasagna."

Both sisters said, "Uh, ummm."

Elaine said, "Kaye, we are going for a walk. An after dinner constitutional is as good as dieting."

Ahlwynn said, "Ah, Mom, do I haf ta."

Elaine said, "No, you don't 'haf ta.'"

Ahlwynn started to look relieved.

His mom continued, "You stay and do the dishes."

Ahlwynn said, "Ah, Mom!"

Kaye said, "Pretend like we are filthy rich, and we demand you help the cook with the dishes."

Ahlwynn said, "A-a-a-g."

He started clearing the dishes as his mom and aunt left for their 'diet constitutional.'

As they went out the door, Kaye glanced up at the sky. "Stormy weather is brewing. Better be a fast walk."

Elaine mumbled something.

As soon as they were out of earshot of the house, Kaye said, "What's up?"

Elaine stared at the ground more than the scenery. "I'm that obvious?"

Kaye said, "When you came out of that restaurant, you walked different. All evening, you've acted like you suddenly have a hearing problem. You kept asking us to repeat everything. What happened?"

Elaine said, "Kaye, I've been a fool. You were right, completely one hundred percent right." She described spotting Edward. "He never made any promises to us; we only shared a couple dinners. He could have said he's a free agent. He lied about being out of town. He wanted us to believe he wasn't seeing anyone else. He deliberately deceived us."

Elaine kicked at a rock in the road. "He's scum."

Kaye said, "I wonder how many women think he isn't dating anyone else. And the worst part is, he never lied! Except for that out of town part. He just let us jump to the conclusion he liked me."

THE MOPSTERS

Elaine thought, *Or liked ME*. She said, "The scheming two-timer did lie! Oh, Kaye, you tried to tell me. I was so wrong."

Kaye said, "You weren't completely wrong. If I'm to get a good man, I need to clean up my act."

Elaine said, "It's more than the lying. Kaye, I was ready to walk all over you to get Edward for myself. Kaye, you were right. I've been alone so long, I wanted what you have. I envied your cute man-getting body; the nights you spent dancing; those special nights when suddenly you know there is no one else in the world, and the only reason for living is to keep that feeling."

Kaye said, "Most guys don't dance all that good. Or know how to make a woman feel like she is the only one in the world." She shook her head. "'Laney, if you have ever had that feeling for real, you are ahead of me." She looked up at her 'dull' older sister. "You have?"

Elaine's eyes went wide as she looked down at her younger sister. "You've not felt like that?"

Kaye said, "No, I've been too busy trying to, oh you know. Sex is fun, but ever make me feel like nothing else exists? Never. You?"

Elaine said, "Every time."

Kaye spoke softly. "Wow."

Elaine said, "I have worried so long, about so much, I thought I could never forget the past, give myself totally over to passion again. Then, I saw Edward, felt his arms, smelled him. Kaye, my body remembered every physical sensation I had the first time...my son's father..." Elaine's voice trailed into silence.

Kaye asked, "Still can't say his name? Yet you say it every time you talk to your son."

Elaine said, "That's different."

Kaye said, "Too bad I was right about Edward. But I'm glad we don't have to fight over who is getting him."

Elaine smiled. "Fight over him? Sister, I am giving him to you. I insist."

Kaye laughed. "Oh, no, that wouldn't be right. You keep him."

Elaine laughed harder. "He is all yours!"

Kaye said, "I felt a raindrop."

Widely spaced large raindrops created big dark circles on the road ahead of them. Kaye asked, "Remember that time we tried to drink the rain, and all we did was get really soaked?"

Elaine leaned her head back, trying to catch raindrops with her mouth. Kaye copied her. Remembering that long ago innocent day, the two women giggled.

The sisters kept laughing as their walk looped back home; Elaine, relieved Kaye took that bad news so well; Kaye, relieved Elaine's new problem wasn't much of problem.

Kaye thought, *Edward was cute enough, but too serious. No one should be taking so many business calls as he did that one night he took me out. Especially if the band is as hot as it was that evening.*

The widely spaced raindrops reminded Elaine of an old song, *'I'll wash that man right out of my hair.' If only…*

They drew near their home. The women saw, parked across the street in the shadows, a pickup truck. The gorilla-men truck.

They stopped laughing.

Episode 14: Up a Tree

Thirty minutes earlier.

Dishes finally washed and drip drying, Ahlwynn went to his room to await Tim's call. He debated about lowering his 'desk' and getting started on his homework, but decided against it.

He left his bedroom light off. His almost closed bedroom door let in a sliver of light from the kitchen. Arms behind his head, Ahlwynn lay on his bed.

Ahlwynn stared out at the night blackness revealed by the narrow window in his room. Thick dark clouds hid the stars. He wished the window opened, but it was painted shut long before his parents bought the house. He studied the swirls of light and dark on his shadowed ceiling.

Alone, he could finally try to think about everything that had happened.

For a day my hat made me so special everyone, even Tim, envied me. I felt like I was better than everyone. But if someone else had worn that hat to school, he would have been better. How can a hat, or a big house, make some people better than other people?

Ahlwynn knew in his gut, without being told, the slobs his mom cleaned up after had to be worse people than those who didn't trash homes. But lately, it seemed some people, like Tim's mom, thought people who owned fancy homes were better than the people cleaning the fancy house. *That is just plain wrong. Figuring out robots is easier than figuring out people, especially adult people.*

The sound of metal jiggling, a creak—-the back door opened.

Ahlwynn listened, anticipating conversation he wasn't supposed to overhear.

Silence.

A soft step.

Strange. Wrong. Danger?

Ahlwynn silently rolled off his bed, stepped near the hinge of his partially open bedroom door. He looked through the crack, thankful the door opened into his room, glad his room was dark, and the kitchen area well lit.

An unfamiliar, tall, bulky man stood by the steel kitchen table. *A burglar!*

Ahlwynn inhaled deeply; his throat felt painfully tight, as though strangled. Every muscle in his body tightened.

The burglar checked out the bathroom. He opened the door to his mom's room.

The stranger walked towards his room. Ahlwynn stood still, holding his breath for fear the man would hear him. The man's shadow darkened Ahlwynn's bed, and the small amount of floor. He seemed to stand there forever.

Ahlwynn's chest hurt; his body screamed silently for air. Ahlwynn feared the burglar could too easily hear him breathe.

A sour smell wafted into the room from the strange man.

Ahlwynn suddenly became aware of the cell phone in his pocket. *What if Tim calls? How can I call for help without moving?* He feared even pulling his phone from his pocket would make too much sound.

Without entering his room, the burglar moved on.

Ahlwynn slowly exhaled, silently inhaled. Carefully, he pulled his phone out, put it on silent alarm.

The burglar glanced into Kaye's room, but headed for the small, cluttered bookcase in the living room area. The man rapidly threw all the books on the floor, opened every box, dumping their contents onto the floor.

THE MOPSTERS

He then went into Kaye's room. From the noise, the burglar was just as thoroughly searching for something of value to steal from Kaye.

Hoping the man was making so much noise he would never hear the door, Ahlwynn ran for the kitchen door. At the door he stopped, slowly opened it to avoid making any excess noise, and carefully, quietly closed it behind him.

Bright yellow light radiated from the wide open garage side door.

Standing in the shadows, Ahlwynn heard the crashing sound of boxes hitting the garage's packed earth floor.

Another burglar?

A bulky man as tall as the one in the house stepped into view. He held a large cardboard box, shook its contents onto the floor. Ahlwynn noticed many other items littered the floor.

Other boxes have been already dumped. Two people are here, ransacking. Are there more?

Ahlwynn knew the men he had seen were not acting like any thief should. He thought of the school trashing. He remembered how his Mom described the trashed houses. Somehow, in some strange way, all of that felt connected.

The streetlight lit path out of his yard looked too open, too vulnerable. Ahlwynn ran for the safer shadows of his tree. Silently, he maneuvered his slender body through the thick branches, heading for his favorite level.

Knowing he was invisible to prying eyes, no matter what kind of flashlights they might have, he stopped. Invisibility felt like a shield.

Fishing out his best binoculars, he searched the street for sign of his mother and aunt. The streetlight on the next block illuminated them. *They're running home! Mom, why exercise now! Mom, stay away!*

Ahlwynn pulled out his phone, speed dialed his mother. He watched through the binoculars, expecting her to stop, to answer. Instead, she ran faster!

Staring at his phone, he said, "I'm a dummy!" He punched 9-1-1.

Careful to pronounce each syllable with extreme precision, he gave his name, his address and that two men who seemed like burglars, but weren't, had broken into his house and garage and were dumping things all over and his mom was running home and she didn't know about the bad guys and could they get a police car, a bunch of police cars, there as soon as possible. Hurry! His mother's life was in danger and the men were really big and really scary and hurry...

The nice sounding lady on the other end interrupted. She repeated the address. "Is that right?"

"Yes!"

"A squad car should be there soon. When will your mother be home?"

"I told you, she's running to the house, any second! If you don't hurry, they will hurt her!"

"I'm putting you on hold, don't hang up."

He was not put on hold; the dispatch lady hung up, but Ahlwynn did not notice. He focused only on his mom and aunt. They were already running around the side of the house, into the backyard.

He heard Kaye scream, "You!" when she saw the man standing in the garage.

His mom screamed, "Ahlwynn!" louder than Ahlwynn had ever heard her scream before.

Episode 15: Vinny

At the same time his cousins screamed fear driven terror, a few miles away Vinny enjoyed the lulling sounds of sophisticated background music.

Unconsciously moving in rhythm to the slow beats of the sedate music, Vinny prepared the special corner table reserved for the exclusive use of the restaurant owner's brother-in-law Alfred, more commonly known as Big Al. Even on extremely busy nights, like tonight, when patrons waited for reserved tables, Big Al's table remained ready for Big Al's exclusive use.

Big Al did not like being interrupted by servers asking if anyone wanted anything. If Big Al had a lot of guests, serving dishes were set on adjacent serving carts, but usually everything was set up 'family style' at his table.

Vinny had worked at Antonio's for over a year before he was finally allowed to serve Big Al's table. Vinny appreciated the prestige as much as he did the '*big-cash*' tips from Big Al's table. Vinny smiled to himself. Tonight was going to be a *big* tip night.

Big Al had called ahead to have his favorite meal ready. He requested even the salad and desserts be part of the family style setup.

Vinny verified the wine carafes, water pitchers and Big Al's personal high capacity Keurig unit were fully stocked and ready to go. Vinny inspected each item of silverware, holding it up to the light, double checking least even a hint of anything remained after going through the commercial dishwasher. If anyone did anything that displeased Big Al, that person no longer worked at Antonio's.

Vinny often wondered, if Big Al wanted so much privacy why didn't he have his meetings in one of the backrooms Antonio rented out for private dinners? Vinny never asked. First day on the job his boss told him, "Never ask why Big Al does anything, or even hint you are curious."

Vinny followed the advice. Others, now gone, didn't.

Vinny started to walk completely around Big Al's table, double verifying its dining-readiness perfection. Vinny glanced down at the floor. Partially hidden by the tablecloth's generous draping, several well-used cloth napkins lay on the floor! *Antonio's clean up crew just lost their jobs!*

Vinny crawled under the table to pick up the offending cloths, glad Big Al had not yet walked in. He had barely knelt down when he heard his boss exclaim, "Alfred! So good to see you! Your table is ready."

Vinny froze. *Is being half under Big Al's table a firing offense?*

He could see a double set of feet, Big Al and someone else, walking past his table, towards the men's room. *Thank goodness I'm next to the wall! He didn't see me!* Vinny did not know he was holding his breath until he started to breathe again.

As Big Al and his companion walked past, Vincent heard him say, "Imagine my shock when I learned the kid's mom was my former cleaning lady. Don't worry, after tonight we need a new cleaning service."

The other man said, "They did good work. You 'firing' them tonight?"

Big Al said, "Any minute now."

The other, almost out of Vinny's earshot, said, "Sending the twins?"

Vinny grabbed the offending napkins, backed out from under the table. He dashed into the kitchen, and almost crashed into his boss. He tossed the napkins into the laundry chute, and rushed back to the dining area.

THE MOPSTERS

The Twins! Vincent didn't have to overhear the rest of the conversation to know in his gut the answer was yes, The Twins were sent. *'Laney, I thought getting you those high paying gigs was a good thing. I thought I was helping you, not getting you killed!*

The last time Vincent's stomach felt the way it did now, someone had sucker-punched him in the gut. *If I leave now, Big Al will assume I know, might even tell those two troglodytes to speed things up. And would order me killed. I can't get my phone from the kitchen without boss man noticing. I have got to warn them! How?*

Vinny remembered the couple in the opposite corner. They had arrived well before the main dinner hour. After taking forever to eat their main course, they now lingered over their dessert. *They've been sitting there for almost three hours. That sometimes happens when folks are dating, especially when the woman is that hot, but neither of them are looking at the other.*

Normally, Vinny would assume a very long meal combined with such stiffness indicated the couple was on a first date, trying to size each other up, but the man had an almost military bearing.

The lady sat in a way he had never seen a woman so skimpily dressed sit.

If the pair weren't first date nervous, there could be another explanation for their body language. *'Laney, if I'm right, maybe, just maybe, you will live.*

Forcing himself to smile, Vinny walked up to the newbie waiter responsible for serving the out-of-place couple, "I noticed table three-B needs more water, but you have an order up. I'll keep dating couple happy, while you serve food to the other table."

The waiter's eyes went wide. Not keeping water glasses full was a firing offense at Antonio's. "Thanks, I didn't notice!" As the newbie headed for the kitchen, he looked back and mouthed, "I owe you."

Grabbing a full water pitcher from the supply table, Vinny headed for the couple. *I hope the new guy has at least one order ready for pick up.*

If not, I can always claim I was confused. Vinny walked quickly, careful to avoid eye contact with the many other patrons.

Both water glasses were almost full. Using his body to block the table from view, Vinny pretended to fill the two water glasses. Vinny looked directly at the man, made full eye contact. "You've been taking a long time eating."

The man's eye's narrowed, but the rest of his face went wooden. "I like the food here."

Vinny, with a hint of a nod, said, "I'm not a virgin waiter; I know customer types. I need to trust someone, to get a message out fast."

The man said, "You think you can trust me?"

Vinny said, "I'm hoping I'm right; you're a fed. You aren't here to eat; you're here to watch, maybe watch for Big Al."

The man's whole body tensed.

Vinny was not surprised to see his companion tense the same way. Vinny said, "Are you?"

The man stared hard at Vinny, "If I am?"

Vinny said, "I need help, not for me. Big Al ordered a hit on my cousins. Tonight. Sending The Twins. My cousins have a small house other side of town, corner of Fourth and Washington."

The man's immediate reaction shocked Vinny. Vinny had heard of all the blood draining from someone's face, but had never before seen it.

The man stood, pulled out his wallet; dropped several hundred dollar bills on the table. Before the bills landed on the table, he was already briskly striding out of the restaurant. His long legs gave his walk running speed.

The sight of the high-heeled redhead chasing after him would have been funny, if Vincent were not so terrified. *I was right, he is a fed on a case, something involving The Twins, 'Lanes, Kaye I'm so sorry.* He pictured his young nephew, all the projects they had done together, Ahlwynn's trusting smile. *I'm so sorry.*

THE MOPSTERS

His hands shaking, Vinny picked up the cash. Forcing himself to breathe deeply, he walked over to the newbie waiter. "Here's payment for three-B's dinner. Looks like a good tip."

The newbie said, "Thanks. They sure left in a hurry."

Vinny said, "He got a text message from one of their kids. Date night ruined again."

Vinny then casually filled water glasses at his regular tables. *Hope no one remembers it was me at that table.*

Several minutes later, Vinny noticed the newbie walking over to Big Al's table. Vinny, carrying a tray full of dirty dishes, walked near. He overheard the newbie say, "Ya, his kid called about some family emergency. He was sure angry date night was ruined again!" Vinny kept walking into the kitchen.

Vinny wanted to keep walking through the kitchen, out into the alley and not stop walking until he was a very long ways away. He knew it would be a very bad idea to do anything out of the ordinary. *Laney-lanes what did you do? Big Al liked your work. He didn't even mind paying you all that extra money. But you did something, something big.*

Vinny kept working. He noted every new person who entered. More than usual, he listened to all conversation in the restaurant.

He tried to not look in the direction of Big Al's table. The more he tried to avoid looking, the more he looked.

The water pitcher again empty, Vinny went to the deep server sink to refill it. He heard boss man tell the head cook, "Tell Vinny he's wanted at Big Al's table." He saw boss man head for Big Al's table.

With silent carefulness, Vincent left the water pitcher in the sink.

While the chef checked an underling's salad arrangement, Vincent headed for the back door. Grabbing his phone from the high shelf near the back door, Vincent walked out into the night.

As he walked down the dark alley, Vincent tried calling Elaine, then Kaye. No answer. He tried Ahlwynn. Straight to voice mail.

F. E. TABOR AND FRAN TABOR

My car's probably safe, but why chance it?
He walked for several blocks before he felt it safe to call a cab. He was relieved the cabby acted bored. Just to be on the safe side, he gave an address several blocks from his cousin's house. Big Al had too many friends.

Episode 16: Mops, Brooms and Bullets!

Stretched out on the high treehouse platform, Ahlwynn stared down on the tableau before him. *Any second now, there will be sirens and police cars and those bad guys will be running away.*

The large man stepped out of the garage, holding something long and dark. He said, "Hello, ladies." In a quiet tone that sounded more dangerous than any yell. "Glad you came home." He slapped one end of the dark thing against his hand. "Perhaps you can help me."

Elaine shouted, "Where's Ahlwynn? Where's my son?"

The man's voice lowered more. He uttered each word as if it were a torture device best used slowly, "Just answer a few questions, and then all your worries will be handled."

Kaye said, "No answers until we get answers."

Elaine, fearing what she might see within, stepped towards the garage door.

Ahlwynn, his fingers gripping the platform's edge, watched. It looked as though the big man barely moved as he slapped his mom.

His mom fell backwards, hard.

He must be strong! When will the cops get here?

The man stepped towards her, saying, "The boss noticed you took a souvenir from your last job. Saw pictures of it on the news. I'm sent to find any other souvenirs, and make sure you never collect another one." The man added, "Real sure."

Ahlwynn's grip tightened. *Souvenir? My hat? Me, in the news? Mom, this is all my fault!*

Ahlwynn understood what the man meant by 'real sure.'

He no longer felt any fear for himself.

Ahlwynn reached for his warrior blowgun, and its special bag of ammunition—-the 'ammo' he and cousin Vinny had made together, the ammo Vinny had made him promise to never show anyone. *Will it work? My special ammo did more than just shred leaves. I've hit dragonflies mid air. I snapped a small branch. Punctured thick wood. Penetrated all the way through eighth-inch plywood.*

Will it really work against a man?

Vinny, we should have made poison for our darts, like those Amazon Indians.

Vinny had drawn a line at making poison.

Ahlwynn leaned against a large branch, inserted a slender, very sharp steel dart into his warrior blowgun, and blew hard.

All those hours practicing paid off. The dart hit hard against the side of the man's neck. It penetrated almost its full length.

"What the—" The man slapped his neck as though the dart had been a mosquito, forcing the dart to penetrate deeper. "Argh!"

He turned, looked up into the thick branches. "Kid, I know you're up there! Come down or—"

Before he could finish speaking, Ahlwynn shot another dart. It hit the man's tongue. Another dart punctured his cheek.

A deep, guttural sound, more animal than human, came out of the man as he charged the tree, thrashing at the branches with the iron bar in his hand. He leaped onto the first platform more gracefully than an over sized thug should be able.

Elaine screamed, "Ahlwynn, higher!" She attempted to stand.

Kaye, seeing a motion out of the corner of her eye, turned to the house. A second man, the second Mr. Strange gorilla, stood there.

He shouted at his partner, "Don't hurt the kid." He bared his teeth. He whispered, "Not yet."

Kaye, staring at him, helped her sister up.

THE MOPSTERS

The first man, the darts pulled from his tongue and cheek, face bleeding heavy, stopped climbing, shouted up into its dark shadows. "That's going to cost you! I was going to go easy on your mom. Now, not so much."

His partner shouted, "Mike, the women."

"Right."

He came out of the tree. The light lit up his blood streaked face. He stepped forward.

The two sisters backed away, towards their vehicle.

Both men grinned at them. Their grins eliminated all trace of humanity.

The women backed up against their station wagon.

Elaine's back pressed against Rusty-Trusty's backdoor. Her hand grasped its handle. *Can I open it; grab something, anything, to use it against him?*

More darts penetrated the nearer man's neck. This time, he was expecting it. This time, he ignored the piercing pain. He took another step forward.

His partner said, "Remember, Boss wants answers."

"I'll get answers." Somehow Mike's 'grin' widened, revealed more teeth. He said nothing, just looked at the two sisters.

The man from the house said, "Wait." He walked over to the tree and shouted up into its thick shadows, "Kid, did you call the police?"

Ahlwynn yelled back, "Yes. You better run. They'll be here any minute!"

The man pulled out a gun, held it so Ahlwynn could easily see it. "What am I holding?"

Ahlwynn said, "A gun."

The man said, "You call the police back, say you were bored, made the whole thing up, no cops needed. You be convincing or..." He aimed the gun at Ahlwynn's mother.

Ahlwynn was surprised to discover he was no longer on hold, but said nothing as he punched the numbers.

The same lady answered.

"This is Ahlwynn. I just called."

"Don't worry, son. The police are coming. It has been a busy night."

Ahlwynn said, "I made the whole thing up. I don't need the police. My mom just got home and she is really, really mad at me for bothering you."

"Are you sure you are all right? Don't you want a squad car sent?"

Ahlwynn said no, please don't bother.

After a couple more reassurances, the dispatcher hung up.

The moment everyone's attention was on the phone call, Elaine opened the Subaru's door. She grabbed the mop. Kaye, realizing what her sister was doing, grabbed the heavy-duty barn broom. Together, they lunged towards the gorilla-men.

The two men turned; kicked the makeshift weapons from their hands.

The bloody one swiped the wooden mop handle with his iron bar, slashing the thin wooden shaft.

The man holding the gun laughed as he stepped back. "Your turn, Mike."

Mike smiled at Kaye; blood dribbled from his mouth. Holding the iron bar over his head, Mike stepped forward.

Elaine grabbed her broken mop handle, shoved its sharp splintered ends into Mike's ribs. It thudded against something hard, skidded up into his armpit. The pole's sharp jags ripped his shirt, tore into his skin.

Ahlwynn shot another razor sharp dart into Mike's back.

Mike shrieked.

His partner laughed harder. "Mike, you scream like a girl."

Mike turned towards Elaine.

Kaye grabbed her broom, rammed the heavy straw end at his eyes.

The stiff straw gouged deep; Mike screamed again.

THE MOPSTERS

His partner laughed even louder.

Mike, one eye blinded, whacked the thick broom handle, snapping it in two as easily as he had the flimsy mop handle. He stepped towards Kaye.

Elaine jabbed her mop into his thigh. No cloth tore. No scream.

Mike twisted away from Kaye, towards Elaine.

Kaye lunged; her heavy-duty, now jagged, broom handle speared into Mike's pants. A dark stain appeared where the shaft penetrated. She jerked the staff out of his flesh.

Mike howled pain.

His mocking partner said, "And you fight like a girl."

Mike pivoted away from Elaine, back to Kaye.

Elaine, a low guttural sound coming from her throat, leaped up, her stick aimed at his throat. He saw the motion, again blocked the broken mop shaft with his crowbar.

Kaye sprung forward, ramming her broken broom handle into his shoulder.

Mike bellowed.

His partner quit laughing. "Enough play." He aimed his gun towards Kaye. "Hey, lady—"

A dart hit his cheek. He screamed. His shot went wild.

The sound echoed thunder between the house and garage.

Elaine gripped her jagged mop handle like a lance.

Every cell in her body adding energy to her deep, primeval yell, Elaine charged into Mike.

This time Mike grabbed the mop with his free hand. Elaine still held it tight. Using her momentum against her, he used the mop handle to flip her back onto the ground.

He hefted his crowbar over his head.

Kaye, her head tucked down, gripping her broom handle like a battering ram, ran full force towards Mike. He kicked her aside without taking his eyes off Elaine.

Elaine stared up. She became intently aware of every detail around her.

The bright rectangle that was the open garage door spilling yellow light into her yard.

The deep shadows cast by layers of tree branches, thick with leaves.

Tree shadows complicated with illumination from the harsh white streetlight, mixing with yellow garage light.

Mixed textures of hardened dirt and patches of grass against her back, a faint smell of old oil.

Light glistening off blue-black metal—a crowbar held high.

Dominating everything, outlined by the garage door's yellow glare, the deep darkness of a hulking man.

Elaine's only thoughts, *When the gun went off, Ahlwynn never screamed. Please Ahlwynn, please be alive. Stay alive.*

Elaine knew she, herself, was about to die.

A white sedan, tires squealing, raced into the yard, doing a tight, dirt-churning turn. A man leaped out, shot the crowbar holding hand. Electric sparks flew from the crowbar.

The second gorilla-man attempted to shoot, another dart hit him; again his shot went wild.

"Freeze! FBI!"

Two black cars followed the white sedan into the yard. The second man dropped his gun.

"Both of you, on the ground! Now!"

They complied.

Men emerged from the other two vehicles.

Ahlwynn jumped down from the tree. "Wow!"

The first FBI agent rushed to Elaine, picked her up, "You OK?"

Elaine looked up into the darkest eyes she had ever seen, felt warm, protecting arms around her; she smelled his comforting man-smell. She demanded, "Who was that redhead?"

"Huh?"

THE MOPSTERS

"I saw you at Antonio's; you were with a slut of a redhead. Who. Is. She."

A woman, wearing an obviously expensive dress that consisted of random bits of shiny red cloth and netting, had emerged from one of the dark sedans. She went to the white sedan, pulled a small briefcase from its backseat.

Her very tall spike heels punctured the lawn as she walked over, but her carriage remained as graceful as if she walked a runway. She said, "That slut would be me, and you must be the infamous Elaine my partner won't shut up about." She glared at Edward. "Not waiting for your partner broke protocol."

Kaye stood. Brushing herself off, she said, "Edward is interested in Elaine?"

Ed's partner nodded. "Interested doesn't begin to describe it."

Kaye eyed the svelte, scantily attired woman. "Does that mean Edward's not a two-timing scumbag after all?"

His partner said, "**Ed** is in the clear. While speeding here, Edward filled us in. You must be The Mob's mystery cleaning crew."

Kaye said, "The what?"

Ahlwynn rushed over. "Did you see that crowbar fly out of that guy's hand? Just like in the movies, only louder!"

Edward's partner said, "Edward, you know what comes next."

Elaine, feeling euphoric, thought, *Ahlwynn's alive. I'm alive. Not just alive, I'm in the arms of my very own prince charming. He wiped out the bad guys, now he's going to wipe out my loneliness, he's—*

Edward's words cut into Elaine's thoughts. "Elaine, I have to arrest you as an accomplice to murder. We don't know what made Big Al turn on you, but he has turned on former accomplices before."

His partner, looking directly at Edward, commanded, "Ed, Her rights."

Edward said, "You have the right to remain silent, to have an attorney."

Kaye shouted, "Bullshit! She's no more guilty than I am."

The partner said, "Funny you should say that." She read the full Miranda rights to both sisters.

Ahlwynn stared at Edward. "I thought you were one of the good guys."

Sirens sounded. A city police car drove up. Two officers got out and walked over to Edward. "We got a report of some shooting here."

Edward said, "I need you to book these two ladies." He whispered to Elaine. "Please trust me."

Elaine said, "What about Ahlwynn?"

Edward said, "I recommend letting him stay in my custody tonight."

Elaine started to say something, stopped herself. She said, "Why do I trust you? Ahlwynn, are you OK with staying with Edward."

Ahlwynn looked at his mom, then at Edward. He looked at the two thugs being handcuffed. *My mom should be getting a medal, not arrested. Something else is happening.* "If you say it's all right, I will."

His mother gave Edward a weird look. "I think the best place for you, at the moment, is with Edward."

The police officers handcuffed Elaine and Kaye. They started to escort them to their squad car, but Edward's partner stopped them. "We may need to ask them questions while we investigate this site."

The two thugs were each escorted into black FBI vehicles.

Several more black sedans drove up to the house. A small army of men emerged from them and started examining everything in the yard, garage and house.

Edward's seductively-attired partner shouted to an agent exiting the house, "OK if I change in there?"

Given the go ahead, she entered the house. She emerged a few minutes later in slacks, shirt and jacket, a badge pinned to her waist. Running shoes replaced her spike heels.

THE MOPSTERS

The transformed partner tossed the briefcase back into Edward's sedan; she strode over to the handcuffed sisters. "I am Agent Kristine Williams."

An exceptionally well-dressed man, breathing hard, ran into the yard. "Ahlwynn! You're alive!"

Ahlwynn yelled, "Vinny!" He dashed into his cousin's arms, hugging him. "Vinny, two men, big men. Vinny, they hurt Mom!"

Vinny hugged Ahlwynn back. "Your mom, is she?" He couldn't finish the sentence.

Ahlwynn answered, "She seems OK, but Vinny, they arrested Mom and Auntie and calling them accessories to murder."

Vincent spotted his two cousins, arms behind their backs, standing between a police car and the redhead from the restaurant. The redhead's military-like stance and changed clothing eliminated all doubt she was as much a 'fed' as the gun-welding man in front of him.

Vinny shouted at Edward. "They ain't no accessories to anything but loving Ahlwynn."

Kristine, focusing on Elaine, told the sisters, "Everyone has a story when things go south and working for Big Al gets dangerous." Her eyes narrowed. She sneered at Elaine, "*You* are the Cleanup Crew Ringleader?"

Edward interrupted, "I didn't say ringleader, I said in charge."

Kristine shrugged her shoulders. "Semantics. I get the kid doesn't know what's going on, but we adults all know these women were being paid for more than cleaning up after a few wild parties."

Vinny said, "No, they didn't. I might have suspected, but no one said anything for certain."

Kaye, her eyes wide, looked from her cousin to Kristine, demanded, "Suspected what?"

Elaine, the bruise on her face darkening, said, "Vinny, I trusted you. Why?"

Vinny said, "You needed money. Big Al talked about family, the young ones out of control. I told myself, no way he would hire an unknown to clean up after something, uh, professional bad. I didn't learn until later his old cleaning crew was part of the problem you cleaned up that first job."

Elaine said, "How long have you known?"

Vinny said, "When you asked for a retainer, when everyone showed up. I knew must be serious. It wasn't hard to figure out."

Elaine charged him, her handcuffed arms behind her. She knocked Vinny to the ground. Elaine landed on him. She kept ramming him with her shoulder. "You could have got Ahlwynn killed!"

Ahlwynn said, "Would have if Edward hadn't shown up. Nine-one-one was useless!"

The two police officers looked at each other. "You called nine-one-one?"

Ahlwynn answered, "Yes, but one of the bad guys forced me to persuade the lady it was a prank call."

An officer said, "We check out all nine-one-one calls, even if convinced they are fake."

The other officer was already in the patrol car, calling dispatch. "Charles is on duty; the regular gal had to go home, sudden stomach flu."

Edward nodded to him. "It's obvious these two women are honest dupes. Uncuff the girls. We'll take it from here." Edward called on his phone, told someone to send an arrest warrant for the 'stomach flu' victim.

Kristine said, "Maybe this time Ed's right. One of our cars will take the girls to our office."

Edward scowled. "If the local nine-one-one office is rigged, what else isn't safe? We keep these witnesses with us."

He nodded at the two officers. "Leave; we'll handle it from here."

THE MOPSTERS

One officer protested; Edward's eyes narrowed. "Your force's corrupt nine-one-one staff almost got this family murdered. You've lost my confidence." They left.

The wind increased, sending a low pitched whistle through the yard. Scattered raindrops again fell, abruptly fell faster and louder. Edward shouted over the rain, "Everyone to the house. Lights off!"

Everybody in, Edward said, "Whatever you were cleaning up after was big enough to warrant rigging a nine-one-one office. Big Al will send others to finish what those two thugs started. Maybe tonight. Lights on, even with shades drawn, we're sitting ducks."

The two sisters, Vinny and Ahlwynn sat on the floor in the dark. The FBI agents checked each window, closed all curtains. They then joined everyone on the crowded living room floor. Each soon learned all the evening's details.

Ahlwynn asked, "Bad guys are out there in *this* rain?"

Edward said, "If even one sniper lurks in the shadows, your mom or aunt could be killed before we even knew they were shot."

Ahlwynn said, "Why kill Mom and Auntie? Anything they remembered could be explained by the stories they were told. Wouldn't that make their testimony useless?"

Edward said, "True. But what if they brought something from one of the fight sites, something that would physically link a victim or a killer to a site? Like a hat only one person owned?"

Ahlwynn said, "Like my hat? The one I wore in the news show?"

Edward said, "Yes."

Elaine said, "But we found the hat outside, covered with mud. It could have blown in from anywhere."

Kristine said, "True, but The Family doesn't know that, or they wouldn't be freaking out so much. Did you take anything else?"

Elaine, Kaye and Vinny all three said, "No, can't think of anything."

Ahlwynn sat silent.

Edward said, "Ahlwynn, you didn't say anything."

Ahlwynn said, "In the movies, if someone gives evidence against bad guys, or the bad guys just think someone has squealed, they are killed. Edward, is that what happens in real life?"

Edward answered, "Sometimes"

Ahlwynn said, "Sometimes, even if the bad guy is arrested, he has friends who will kill anyone who helped get him arrested. That's a true for reals, too, isn't it?"

Edward said yes, it was.

Ahlwynn said, "Someone who would send those two bad guys to kill my mom without even bothering to find out if she had really done anything to hurt him, someone like that must be really bad."

Edward said, "Really bad."

Ahlwynn started to cry. "I bet witness protection plans are for real too. But I bet they only work if you have a real witness, not just someone the bad guys think might be a witness. Right?"

Edward didn't answer.

Ahlwynn asked again, "You need real, for sure evidence. Right?"

Kristine said, "Right, kid. Witness protection money is only for witnesses. But if you can come up with a bit of real evidence, more than the hat, we can get you, your cousin, aunt and Mom relocated to a brand new place in a brand new town in a brand new state. Would you like to live where it snows?"

Ahlwynn said, "I like my house. I love my school. I have a friend, a real friend for the first time in my life. I don't want a new life, but I don't want bad guys to ever hurt my mom again. If we have real evidence, can you promise my mom won't get hurt?"

Edward spoke softly, "Promise? No, I can't promise. But it's the best chance your mom has."

Ahlwynn said, "We have evidence somebody bled, a lot, at the first house Mom cleaned."

Elaine said, "Kaye cleaned that table real good, with soap and water."

THE MOPSTERS

Ahlwynn said, "It was upside down when whoever was hurt bled into it. It pooled in it. The wood on the bottom, the upside down part, was raw wood, no finish. The blood soaked into it. It's still stained. That's why I put cork board over it, to use it like a bulletin board. I didn't like being reminded some raccoon killed a cat; that someone's pet bled to death there."

Elaine said, "That stain isn't enough to blood type, identify the killer."

Edward said, "Ahlwynn's right. It is enough. Where's the table?"

Ahlwynn said, "On the wall in my room."

Edward and Kristine started laughing. Vinny asked what was so funny.

Edward said, "Big Al sent his two most thorough thugs. The FBI sent a trained crew. All to hunt for something, anything that would link the sisters to murder sites. All the time, it was a giant, framed bulletin board in a kid's room, hidden in plain site."

Kristine said, "Looks like your witness protection starts right now."

Ahlwynn said, "I can't wait to tell Tim what happened! That my mom is helping the FBI solve a big case!"

Edward said, "Hand me your phone."

Ahlwynn handed it to him.

Edward took out the battery, handed it back to him. "Your former friends will never learn how brave you were tonight. They will be told your mom could not afford to keep you in Kathy's School. She went through a bankruptcy, lost her home and cell phones, had moved to live with an aunt back in Mexico."

Ahlwynn said, "We don't look Mexican."

Kristine said, "People from all over the world live in Mexico, just like the United States."

Ahlwynn said, "But really, we'll be going someplace it snows?"

Kristine said, "Yes, eventually. First, we need to send the table top to a laboratory. Have your family in custody, have court hearings. But this is the last day you will spend here."

Ahlwynn jumped up, screamed, "No! It's not fair! I don't want to leave! This is where Dad lives!"

He ran out of the house.

Elaine ran after him, "Ahlwynn! It's not safe!"

Ahlwynn ran into the night.

His mother saw where he ran; dreaded hearing a gunshot that did not come.

Edward started to run after him. Elaine stopped him. "He's already in his tree. No one can see him. He needs to be there. Right now, he needs to be in his tree."

The garage light off, the tree loomed dark. It appeared to be a perfect hiding place, but to anyone with an infrared scope, Ahlwynn would show up as vividly as if he had a search light focused on him.

Edward started to tell Elaine about infrared scopes. Looking at her face, he asked, "You know the risks?"

Elaine nodded yes. "All the times Ahlwynn felt like a freak, like he was the only one like him in the whole world, he would climb that tree; go up it a scared child. Later, sometimes minutes, sometimes hours, he would come down, a normal, adventurous boy. Edward, you can protect his body. Can you, can anyone, protect his spirit?"

Edward said, "Ahlwynn told me how important that tree is to him, how it makes him think of his father."

Elaine looked up at him. *He understands, he accepts...how could I ever have doubted Edward's goodness?*

AHLWYNN CLUTCHED THE shadow-shrouded tree trunk. The few raindrops that made it through the tree's thick leaves blended with his tears.

THE MOPSTERS

"Dad, they want to take me away from you. No one understands. No one else knows. Dad, I know you are here."

Ahlwynn didn't need light to know where the heart was. He didn't need light to know where the initials were.

His fingers found the deep impressions, traced the letters.

A H + E B

He traced the letters over and over.

He traced the heart.

A wind gust whirled through the tree. Branches whipped against each other.

Rain pelted Ahlwynn from every direction at once.

The twisting winds shook the massive tree as though it were a small weed. Shaking branches violently jerked Ahlwynn's many 'cubby holes'; the wind's howling crescendo clashed into the clanging of Ahlwynn's 'wind chimes.'

A book crashed onto a branch next to Ahlwynn; he rescued it. *Dad, it's Treasure Island! Your book!* Holding the book tightly, Ahlwynn visualized its old message, 'Adventure begins when you leave home.'

He looked up. "Dad, you're right. It is time." He tucked the book inside his shirt. He climbed out of the tree.

A branch rubbed against him. He gripped the branch, rubbed it against his cheek. Ahlwynn said, "Mom told me you said the secret to living is adventure."

As he stepped away from the tree's protective umbrella, overhead lightning leaped from cloud to cloud.

Thunder rumbled.

A heart beat of silent darkness.

Bam!

Thunder wrapped Ahlwynn teeth-quaking tight; lightning ripped overhead.

F. E. TABOR AND FRAN TABOR

Ahlwynn ran back into the house. "Vinny, let's get that table off my wall, now!" He looked around the small kitchen-living room; he remembered laughter filled days. "Mom, we gotta leave."

His mother looked at him. "I know."

Edward said, "I'll help Vinny get the table top off the wall. Elaine, you and your sister, grab a few things to take with you."

Edward helped Vinny jerk the table top off the wall. The two men ran the tabletop to Edward's sedan.

A massive lightning bolt struck the garage; another bolt hit the house.

Smoke smell filled the air. Loud, crackling sounds surrounded the car.

Many layers of old roofing on the dilapidated garage burst into flame; each layer curled up. Fourth-of-July quality sparks filled the air, but both men ignored them.

Both focused on the tiny house.

A roaring conflagration exploded from its roof. Black smoke, white flames, orange...

Both men ran towards hell.

THE FOLLOWING DAY THERE was a picture in the local paper of a lone tree standing between two blackened rectangles on the ground; all that remained of an ancient garage and house. The caption beneath it read:

The fire consumed the poorly built house so fast all three family members died. Next Wednesday the child's school will host a celebration of life.

Episode 17: Kathy's Tale

One month later

Edward knocked on Kathy's office door as he let himself in. "Working late again, Sis?"

Before she could answer, he said, "Thought so. I brought our favorite meals." He held up a sack from their childhood favorite fast food. The sinfully enticing aroma of cheap fries and hamburgers filled the office. He pulled out two cartoon-covered boxes. "Remember; eat every bite before you open the toy."

Kathy said, "I tell my students to eat healthy." She moved her keyboard aside to make room for the box. Grabbing a large envelope from her trash to protect her desk, she put the box onto her makeshift placemat. Edward placed her soda next to it, and sat across from her. Following her lead, he pulled another paper from her trash and used it for his placemat.

Edward said, "You have been working over-long hours ever since the funeral."

Kathy opened up her box. She sniffed the salty greasy fries. She took her first bite. "Uh, hot!" She flipped the plastic lid off her drink and gulped.

Edward smiled. "All these years, you still haven't learned to blow on the first fry." He pulled out his first, hot fry and puffed on it. He bit off the tip. "Mmmmmm."

He quit smiling. "Katherine, working so many excess hours is like drinking. It only seems like it is helping."

Kathy nodded as she ate. "I know, but life is so unfair. Ahlwynn had so much potential. He wasn't just bright, he was sweet and imaginative. He had a maturity to him. I kept thinking of him as a bright twelve year old, not ten. Edward, I meet a child like him about once every five years, if that often. What could he have done if he had lived? You know what's worse?"

Edward, deliberately eating slowly, said, "No. What's worse?"

Kathy said, "Just the day before he died, I got to know a little more about Ahlwynn's mother. I don't care what she felt compelled to do to keep her home, protect her son. Edward, I liked her. I would have been proud to have her as a sister-in-law."

Edward said, "I was sure you would feel like that, eventually. I'm glad you got to see a glimpse of the real her."

Kathy said, "Speaking of real, can you believe how that Ms. Charley carried on? She must have spoke nearly an hour about how Ahlwynn was one of the best students she ever had, how sad she was when Ahlwynn's mom pulled him out of public school, but she understood. After all, it was her recommendation that led Elaine into looking for schools better suited for the unusually bright child he was."

She picked up the foil ketchup packet. She squeezed it so hard the ketchup overshot the remaining fries and landed on her makeshift placemat. "Ed, along with the usual application papers, Elaine shared the reports Ms. Charley wrote about Ahlwynn. Elaine believed she needed to warn me her son was 'different.' Ed, you would not believe the garbage that woman wrote about little Ahlwynn!"

Elaine jabbed her next fry so hard into the ketchup mound it smashed. "Watching that woman completely change her tune, I wanted to stand up and holler 'Liar!' loud enough people three states away could hear me. Instead, I just sat there, properly quiet."

Kathy ate her mutilated fry. She ate each of the remaining fries just as violently.

THE MOPSTERS

Edward said, "Maybe Charley's feelings were more honest at the funeral? At any rate, she helped create a better memory about Ahlwynn for the children."

Kathy said, "I suppose." Her fries finished, she started in on her hamburger. "You remembered the extra pickle!"

Edward said, "For my favorite sister, everything!"

Kathy said, "Remember how I thought it was so funny when Dad would say, 'You're in a pickle.' And I would get mad at him because that was such a stupid expression. Pickles are too small to put a person inside them."

Edward laughed. "The more you protested, the more times he found to use that expression."

Kathy said, "Does anyone even say that anymore?"

Edward shrugged. "You're the teacher. You tell me. Does anyone?"

Kathy said, "Ed, the vandalism day, the day Ahlwynn died, I had put myself into an ugly pickle. You know what I regret the most about his death? It is a totally selfish regret, all about me, not him. I regret not getting to see the expression on Charlene's face when I told her to shove her demands where the sun doesn't shine. I didn't care if I never saw her or her spoiled brat children again. I didn't care what she said about me to my face or behind my back, I didn't care if I lost the school, my home, my car and everything else I owned, I didn't care about any of that. Ahlwynn was staying. He was a good student, had done nothing wrong, I was not expelling him."

Edward said, "Whoa! Back up a little. What are you talking about?"

Kathy said, "Remember that text I sent you? About the school mystery?"

Edward said, "Vaguely. We were all a little busy when the house fire was discovered. When I saw how little of the bodies remained... Kathy, Elaine was an unusual person. I wanted to marry her in the middle of that first dinner at her house. If you could have seen the way, the whys, of her smiles. The way her body moved when putting food on the table; her quiet unassuming pride in a job well done. Her house was truly 'thread-bare', but the book shelf was full of well-used books. He son at home was happy, the kind of secure happy that says he knows he is loved. Kathy, I love Elaine."

Kathy said, "I know you did. But you would have quit loving me if you knew what I almost did."

Edward watched his sister finish the last of her hamburger. Just like when they were children, she rolled up the hamburger wrapper into a tight ball which she shoved into the small fry bag. She dropped that into the carton and removed the plastic toy.

She stared at the figure. "Edward, I teach children and I have no idea if this character is one of the good guys or one of the bad guys. The day of the vandalism, I discovered my good and bad guy labels for people were totally screwed up. Worse, Ed, I almost became one of the bad guys."

In a rush, Kathy described her meeting with Charlene, how Charlene left 'knowing' she was going to get exactly what she wanted.

Kathy said, "Edward, after she left I felt like I died, like she had killed me, like my school was already dead. That's when it hit me. She used the vandals as an excuse for what she wanted when she first came in. It didn't make sense. Charlene is one of those super-friendly sophisticated types; nothing fazes her. Suddenly she is Boston Puritan. Something didn't ring right. That not-right feeling opened me up to my own feelings. If keeping the school open meant open on terms that made it feel dead, what kind of open is that? I chose to not call Elaine. I was not going to expel Ahlwynn. I felt so self-righteously powerful."

Kathy sat up straighter. "I was going to tell Charlene to her face, to take her trashy butt out of my school, to never darken the halls with her presence again! Now, I have lost forever the chance to tell her off."

Edward, taking his last bite, said, "Why? You can still tell her you changed your mind. Ahlwynn was staying."

THE MOPSTERS

Kathy shook her head, "No, I can't. She would no more believe me, than I believe Ms. Charley had a change of heart."

Edward crumbled up his wrappers the same way his sister did and shoved them into his meal box. He collected his toy figurine. He returned the box to its plain paper bag. "You're right, she wouldn't believe you. Want me to get rid of the evidence you didn't eat healthy?"

Kathy said, "Please do." She handed him her wrapper filled box.

Carefully folding over her ketchup stained 'placemat' envelope, she shoved it deep into the wastebasket, hiding it amongst the office trash paper. "Edward, I've heard Charlene is thinking of moving to a larger city, with more opportunities. She can't leave fast enough for me."

Edward, one eyebrow raised, asked, "When did you hear that?"

Kathy said, "I overheard her talking during the social after Ahlwynn's Celebration of Life."

Edward, with a slight frown, "Did you get a hint of such plans, or any desire to move before then? Even a suggestion our city isn't large enough for her ambitions?"

Kathy said, "No, not at all. Just the opposite." Kathy recognized the look on her brother's face. "Will you tell me why that's important, or is it too important?"

Edward said, "I don't know. Tell me everything you know about her."

Kathy did, all the while wondering which piece of information made Charlene suddenly so very interesting to her brother.

Edward nodded. "I think it's a good thing we had this talk." He put his toy next to his sister's. "Sis, being one of the good guys isn't a decision made once for all time. Unlike these guys." He moved the two plastic cartoon creatures as though they were walking together. "We don't have a script telling us our lines. Sometimes we say or do the wrong thing. Sis, I know, had Ahlwynn lived, you would have done the right thing." Taking the incriminating fast food cartons with him, Edward left.

AN HOUR LATER EDWARD was calling on a secure line. "Hi, Elaine?"

"Edward!"

"Elaine, do you remember Charlene, one of the mothers from Kathy's School?"

Elaine said, "Charlene? No, but I only met a couple of the moms."

Edward could hear her shout to someone else in the room. "Hey, do either of you remember a Charlene?"

Kaye grabbed the phone, "Charlene and Richard Fox?"

Edward said, "Yes."

Elaine was in the background. "We do? Who are they? Put the phone on speaker."

Kaye said, "They are the reason we showed up at the open house."

Edward said, "You knew *them?*"

Elaine asked, "How do you know it was their house?"

Kaye said, "Remember, I told you they had bills on the counter. Those bills had their name on them, duh."

Edward said, "Their house for what?"

Elaine said, "One of our cleaning assignments."

Kaye said, "They had bills on their kitchen counter, one of them for Kathy's school, and an open house invitation rested on top of their kitchen trash. I recycled the invitation out of their garbage. Unless, like my silly sister, you call garbage swiping stealing. Then, maybe I stole it."

Edward said, "Have you discussed that with an agent?"

Elaine said, "No, the interviewers were only interested in the two jobs we had evidence from. They let me know my duty is to answer the questions they ask."

Edward mumbled something about beginners. "Elaine, Kaye, I am listening. Tell me everything you remember about the Fox house, from

THE MOPSTERS

the time you drove up the driveway to the time you drove away. Don't leave out anything."

For the next two hours, they talked. The more the sisters talked, the more they remembered.

Edward thanked them, said they gave him new information that will help track down additional leads. For the first time, he had a clue who Big Al's 'legitimate' business connection might be.

As Edward hung up the secure landline phone, he thought, *If Alice hadn't gone gossiping, telling everyone my Elaine was a hooker, that bitch Charlene would never have known Ahlwynn attended her daughters' school. Charlene must have assumed they worked for Big Al. She would have been terrified Elaine or Kaye might recognize her at a school function and reveal her underworld connections.*

Charlene, you threatened my sister and tried to ruin Elaine and Ahlwynn's lives. I bet you felt thankful when all three "died" in the fire. Charlene, your days of ruining other people's lives are numbered.

A YEAR LATER, EDWARD gave a talk at both Ahlwynn's old school and at Kathy's School about how Big Al was finally behind bars because of Ahlwynn's mother. She worked as an undercover agent for the FBI. Some agents believed Big Al did something to her house to make it more vulnerable to a lightning strike. It couldn't be proved. Because of the information Elaine and Kaye provided before that fateful night, Big Al was proved guilty of other murders.

Ahlwynn not only knew the risk his mother took, he had bravely helped her with some of the undercover work.

Privately, with the adults, Edward revealed the rumors Elaine and Kaye engaged in prostitution were false; those rumors were part of their undercover persona.

Edward felt a special smug pride when he overheard Alice tell one of her friends, "I could always tell Elaine was something special. She was one of my dearest friends."

Edward also felt an emptiness. It had been months since his final conversation with Elaine. His final conversation because he knew of too many case files marked 'Terminated. Dead.' that happened when a brief postcard or quick phone call announced to the world "Witness Not Dead." Nothing, absolutely nothing, would make him ever put Elaine and her family into so much jeopardy.

Episode 18: New Beginnings

Three years later

Cynthia Bowman sat at her office desk, opening the day's mail for her boss, the director of a prestigious but cash-strapped private school for the gifted in the middle of North Dakota.

Cynthia had worked hard to develop the secretarial, bookkeeping and janitorial skills required for her ombudsman position.

She had trouble adjusting to North Dakota's harsh weather, but her sister Alicia and Cousin Benny took to it as though they had been born in a blizzard.

Her son Alfred enjoyed the school; he had made friends. But a little too often he would stare at nothing in particular, like he was looking for something not there.

Cynthia understood how he felt. She did the same thing.

Cynthia sighed. She didn't want to admit it to anyone, but her baby sister was right. It was time to stop dreaming about an almost-romance and take a chance on real life. The recently-widowed insurance agent who called on the school had been trying to get her to go to lunch with him. He wasn't bad looking; maybe she should. Feeling dating would be unfaithful to an FBI agent she would never see again was worse than foolish; it was beyond stupid.

One of the letters she opened was an application for a newly created teaching position. The man had been a deputy sheriff in a small Texas border town, suffered burnout, now he wanted to try teaching. She put his resume with the others the school had already received.

F. E. TABOR AND FRAN TABOR

Cynthia was sure her boss would turn him down. They had only the one teacher opening, and so many better qualified applicants.

Cynthia went into her boss's office. "Here are all the résumés for your new teaching position."

He took the papers from her, handed all but one application back to her. "Send these people regrets, but the position has been filled."

"Already? Who did you pick?"

A voice from behind answered, "Me. Let me introduce myself, I'm Robert Sanderson, former deputy sheriff from the land of sand and armadillos, ready to tackle the grass and jackrabbits of North Dakota."

Cynthia turned. She looked up into the warmest, darkest eyes she had ever seen in a man. "Robert Sanderson?"

The former lawman smiled. "That's right."

Cynthia smiled back. "Robert, since you are new in town, would you like to come over to my house for some old fashion Italian cooking? My sister, cousin and son will be there."

"If you let me help. I can chop vegetables with the best of them."

Cynthia knew she was never going to date the insurance man.

That evening, her son learned he had someone with whom he could talk about his old life, his new life and how a father's love is never pretend.

Being a fledgling teenager, and therefore wise in the ways of the world, Alfred was not surprised when his mom married the handsome 'Texan', or that they soon had a little girl.

Like his mother had her little sister Alicia, at last he, too, had a little sister. Alfred read bits of Treasure Island to his sister almost every night from the first day she was home from the hospital.

Alicia opened a cleaning business. She quit when she married her favorite client.

Benny taught a local elderly restaurant owner how to "put some class in the joint." By the time his cousin Cynthia had "finally put

THE MOPSTERS

Robert out of his misery and married the poor sucker" Benny owned the place.

The following year, Benny invited his whole family—-his cousins and their husbands, nephew, new niece—-to enjoy an on-the-house dinner to help him celebrate his first full year of owning the finest dining establishment in all of North Dakota.

As Alfred walked into Benny's restaurant, he looked up at his cousin's new sign. Like he did every time he looked at it, Alfred thought, '*That is the biggest change in our family.*'

Benny used the outline of his massive mustache and goatee as the symbol for his restaurant, New Beginnings.

Also by F. E. Tabor

The Mopsters
Eagle Rock

Watch for more at https://www.amazon.com/author/fran-tabor.

Also by Fran Tabor

The Mopsters
To Own Two Suns

Watch for more at https://www.amazon.com/author/fran-tabor.

About the Author

This book was inspired by all the hardworking, self-employed people Fran has been honored to know, and by their wonderful children.

Read more at https://www.amazon.com/author/fran-tabor.

Printed in the USA
CPSIA information can be obtained
at www.ICGtesting.com
CBHW020000201024
16068CB00003B/97